Wade's feelings were growing deeper.

He was attracted to Dixie, and had examined his feelings for her for days. In addition, there was respect, admiration and a strong liking, different from anything he'd felt for anyone else.

This was a man-woman liking.

The boys… He didn't have to examine his feelings for them. He flat-out loved them, no two ways about it. He didn't think it mattered whether the feeling came from himself, or from the new heart beating in his chest. The heart was his now.

Whatever he felt, it came from him—
Wade Harrison.

WINNING DIXIE

JANIS REAMS HUDSON

SPECIAL EDITION®

Published by Silhouette Books

America's Publisher of Contemporary Romance

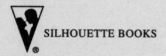 SILHOUETTE BOOKS

ISBN 0-373-24763-X

WINNING DIXIE

Copyright © 2006 by Janis Reams Hudson

All rights reserved. Except for use in any review, the reproduction or utilization of this work in whole or in part in any form by any electronic, mechanical or other means, now known or hereafter invented, including xerography, photocopying and recording, or in any information storage or retrieval system, is forbidden without the written permission of the editorial office, Silhouette Books, 233 Broadway, New York, NY 10279 U.S.A.

All characters in this book have no existence outside the imagination of the author and have no relation whatsoever to anyone bearing the same name or names. They are not even distantly inspired by any individual known or unknown to the author, and all incidents are pure invention.

This edition published by arrangement with Harlequin Books S.A.

® and TM are trademarks of Harlequin Books S.A., used under license. Trademarks indicated with ® are registered in the United States Patent and Trademark Office, the Canadian Trade Marks Office and in other countries.

Visit Silhouette Books at www.eHarlequin.com

Printed in U.S.A.

Books by Janis Reams Hudson

Silhouette Special Edition

Resist Me If You Can #1037
The Mother of His Son #1095
His Daughter's Laughter #1105
Until You #1210
*Their Other Mother #1267
*The Price of Honor #1332
*A Child on the Way #1349
*Daughter on His Doorstep #1434
*The Last Wilder #1474
†The Daddy Survey #1619
†The Other Brother #1626
†The Cowboy on Her Trail #1632
**Winning Dixie #1763

*Wilders of Wyatt County
†Men of the Cherokee Rose
**Tribute, Texas

JANIS REAMS HUDSON

was born in California, grew up in Colorado, lived in Texas for a few years and now calls central Oklahoma home. She is the author of more than twenty-five novels, both contemporary and historical romances. Her books have appeared on the Waldenbooks, B. Dalton and BookRak bestseller lists and earned numerous awards, including the National Reader's Choice Award and Reviewer's Choice awards from *Romantic Times BOOKclub*. She is a three-time finalist for the coveted RITA® Award from Romance Writers of America and is a past president of RWA.

To organ donors. You precious few who decide in advance to leave your organs to others when you no longer need them. There is a special place in heaven for each of you.

Prologue

Wade Harrison was a man used to controlling every-thing and everyone around him. Now he couldn't lift his own hand from the bed. He'd gone from being CEO of his family's vast media empire to helpless invalid.

Scratch that. Helpless invalid would be a step up. He was dying. Unless a matching heart donor was found, and soon—maybe this very night if the look on his mother's face was any indication—Wade was going to die.

And wasn't that a ghoulish thought, wishing some poor slob would die so he could live? Ghoulish, selfish and inevitable, because he didn't want to die.

He knew God, or the universe, or whatever or whomever a person believed in, didn't work on the barter system, but if any of them did, Wade figured there wasn't much he wouldn't promise one or all of them to get another chance at life.

Not that he'd done such a bad job of it in his thirty-four years—Jeez, whoever heard of a thirty-four-year-old heart transplant patient? Damned viral infection, anyway. A *virus*. Like a stupid cold in his heart, and now his heart was quitting on him. And there were still things he wanted, things that had nothing to do with his success in the corporate world. He'd never had a family of his own. Never learned to play the guitar. Never owned a dog.

A dog, for crying out loud? He sincerely hoped he got a heart soon, or went ahead and died before he drowned himself in a pool of self-pity.

On the sidewalk outside Madison Square Garden, Jimmy Don McCormick of Tribute, Texas, flipped his cell phone shut and swore at himself. When it came to his wife and kids—make that ex-wife and kids—he couldn't do a dang thing right. He'd called to talk to his boys, but it was nearly midnight and they'd been sound asleep.

"Shoulda called earlier," he muttered to himself.

But at least Dixie promised to give them a hug from him and tell them he had called. That was something.

He blinked to focus his vision. How much had he had to drink, anyway? Damn good thing the bronc riding event wasn't until tomorrow, or he'd be in a world of hurt.

But tomorrow, by God, Jimmy Don McCormick was going to bust a bronc in Madison Square Garden in New York City, he was.

The curb looked like it was moving. Like a Texas sidewinder. Jimmy thought a snaking curb was pretty funny. He burst out laughing and stumbled off the curb and into the street…directly into the path of an oncoming taxi.

A few minutes later, while one cop took a statement from the devastated taxi driver, the other officer pulled the wallet from the pocket of the newly deceased. "Poor idiot," he muttered. "James Donald McCormick. Came all the way from Texas just to donate his organs."

Around noon the next day Wade Harrison woke from his surgery. Groggy and not yet fully aware of having a new heart donated by a stranger, he blinked his eyes open and tried to lick his lips, but he was still on the ventilator and couldn't get his dry tongue around the plastic hose that fed air into his lungs.

"He's waking up."

Wade squinted and tried to bring the blond hair

and pale face into focus, but it took too much energy. Besides, he would recognize his mother's voice anywhere, anytime.

"Oh, son." His mother leaned down and kissed his cheek. "The surgery's over, and according to your doctor it was textbook perfect."

Wade drifted back into the darkness. When he woke again, some time must have passed, since they'd taken him off the ventilator.

"Are you thirsty?" His mother leaned over him. "I can let you suck on some ice chips."

"Thanks," he managed. "Hug my two best boys for me."

His vision was clearing enough for him to register his mother's look of confusion. She frowned, and it was a good one; she was a champion frowner. "What boys, dear?"

Wade blinked again. "Dunno. What boys?"

"You just said something about hugging your boys."

"Boys?" He had no idea what she was talking about, but he suddenly felt incredibly sad. "Who's gonna hug them now?"

"Doctor?" Alarm filled his mother's voice. "Something's wrong."

Chapter One

It had been a long two years, but Wade Harrison was grateful for every second of that time. He was lucky to be alive, and he knew it. He knew, too, that he wouldn't have survived if not for the death of a stranger and his generous gift. He owed his life not only to his team of doctors, nurses and therapists, but also to a man named James Donald McCormick, who'd had the guts to sign an organ donor card.

Wade wasn't supposed to know the name of the man whose heart now beat inside his chest, but money and tenacity could find out just about anything, and Wade had plenty of both and wasn't ashamed to use either. The least he could do was make certain McCormick's family was getting along all right.

Funny, he thought as he stood on Main Street in Tribute, Texas, and looked up at the neon sign that read Dixie's Diner. He hadn't been this nervous when he'd chaired his first board meeting, yet here he stood, palms sweaty and stomach jumpy. To give himself a minute, he plunked coins into the machine just outside the café door for a copy of the local paper.

Stupid, really, this unusual case of nerves. He slapped the *Tribute Banner* against his leg. No one needed to know who he was or why he was here. He had every intention of remaining anonymous. Hang around town long enough to find out how McCormick's boys were doing—two of them, he'd learned—then head home. A day or two at most.

With a calming breath he pushed open the door to Dixie's Diner and stepped inside. A small bell over the door dinged, announcing his entrance.

The smell of frying meat dominated the air. The decor was 1950's highway-gas-station chic, with old Burma Shave, service station and U.S. 66 signs covering the walls and hanging from the ceiling. Booths lined the front and one side wall, chrome-legged tables and chairs filled the open floor, and a counter with chrome bar stools separated the dining area from the work area and kitchen.

Business appeared to be light, but it was only

11:30 a.m. The lunch crowd, if there was such a thing in this small Texas town, could fill the place up soon. Currently fewer than a dozen customers sat scattered throughout the dining room, two here, three there and one old man in faded overalls at the counter.

Wade didn't think he'd ever actually seen a person in bib overalls before. He supposed that made him a city boy, and he silently acknowledged that the name fit.

The woman who exploded from the kitchen through the swinging doors drove all thoughts of city versus country out of Wade's mind. She wasn't the most beautiful woman he'd ever seen, although she was beautiful. Her shoulder-length hair, dark blond with lighter streaks, was mussed, and her makeup was long gone. She wore a dishtowel around her waist as an apron, and a red plastic name tag over her breast that read Dixie. And her eyes were blue enough to drown in.

No, it wasn't her looks or her clothes that struck him dumb. It was the warm, soft feeling in his chest, the feeling of…familiarity. Which was crazy, since he'd never seen her before.

From his research—and that name tag—he knew this was Dixie McCormick, the ex-wife of his donor, mother of his donor's sons.

Wade was convinced it was McCormick's sons he had felt so anxious about when he'd awakened from the transplant surgery two years ago. Cellular memory, they called it. The medical community still debated whether or not such a thing existed, but a sizable number of transplant patients knew the feeling of waking up from surgery and wanting or knowing or feeling something that could come from nowhere else but the organ donor.

Hug my two best boys for me.

Those words had burst inside Wade's head and tumbled from his mouth the instant they had removed the breathing tube from his throat a day after his surgery, before he had been aware of what he was saying.

Now the mother of those two boys noticed him and came to an abrupt halt. "Hello."

It took him a moment, but he finally unstuck his tongue from the roof of his mouth. This should be simple enough. He was used to addressing directors' meetings, shareholders' meetings, stingy bankers, politicians. He was good at speaking with people. He opened his mouth and out came, "Hi."

Great. Brilliant.

He made a helpless gesture with his folded newspaper.

The woman's eyes widened. She placed her pitcher of iced tea on the counter. "Oh. The paper. You're here about one of the jobs."

Wade looked down at the paper in his hand. "The jobs."

"Thank God." She rushed toward him and extended a hand. "I'm Dixie McCormick." Hers was not the hand of a pampered society princess. It was too strong, too rough and work worn.

He didn't want to let go. There was a connection there, beyond the obvious of hand to hand. Something deeper, more elemental. He might have blamed it on cellular memory, but something told him he'd be wrong. "Wade," he finally managed. "Harrison."

"Wade Harrison." She pulled her hand free and smiled broadly. "You'll have to pardon me for saying so, but you don't exactly look like you need a job."

Wade glanced down at his clothes. He hadn't wanted to stand out, so he'd worn his faded jeans and running shoes, but he hadn't wanted to look sloppy, either, so he'd topped them with a white dress shirt tucked in at the waist.

"I have a T-shirt with a hole in it," he offered, "but…" *Think Texas.* "I use it to wash my truck. And clean my gun."

"In that case," she said, laughing, "I'm glad you didn't wear it. But you can't wash dishes or grill burgers and steaks in a white dress shirt. And pardon me again, but you don't look much like a dishwasher or a short-order cook. Where are you from?"

Wade shrugged. "Here and there." It wasn't a lie. Sure, he had an apartment in Manhattan, but there was the condo in Aspen, the beach house on Maui, and the family compound on Martha's Vineyard. "New York, most recently."

"A traveling man, huh? And you want to work

here." She made it into a statement rather than a question. A statement she didn't seem to believe.

When he had walked through the door a few minutes earlier, it hadn't occurred to Wade to use the excuse of needing a job to hang around and check on McCormick's sons, yet here was the man's ex-wife, offering him employment. It was too good an opportunity to pass up.

"Why not?" he asked her. "A man has to eat."

She looked him up and down again, then shook her head. "Let me see your hands."

"My hands?"

"Yes. Palms up."

Wade tucked the newspaper beneath his arm and held his hands out, palms up, suddenly grateful for time spent on the tennis court.

She grasped his hands and ran her thumbs over the slight calluses along the pads of the fingers of his right hand. "Well, I guess you've done some work before."

He just shrugged. "I've worked." Not manually, not for many years, but he'd worked his butt off in more than one boardroom. He thought it ironic that playing tennis, which he did to relax, would turn out to be more important in getting him a job than having been CEO of the nation's largest media conglomerate. The latter had not put calluses on his hands.

"Were you interested in night cooking or daytime dishwashing?"

While he could cook—he was a bachelor and

didn't like to starve—he doubted his repertoire matched the diner's menu. Also, the woman before him was the key to the boys he was looking for, and she obviously worked days. Sticking as close to her as possible seemed his best bet.

"Daytime dishwashing," he told her. He only had to do it long enough to get a handle on McCormick's boys. A few days at most.

She stared at him for a minute, doubt furrowing her brow. Then finally, when he was about ready to squirm like the only kid in class who hadn't finished his homework, she gave a nod and took him by the arm.

"All right, I'll give you a try." She led him behind the counter, through the swinging doors and into the kitchen. "Not that I think you've ever washed a dish in your life," she muttered just loud enough for him to hear. Then, louder, "Pops, help is here. This is Wade. Wade, Pops. He'll show you around."

Pops was a wiry, gray-headed old man with more wrinkles on his face than anyone had a right to. He stood maybe five-five on legs so bowed he looked as if he might still be straddling a horse. No telling how tall he'd be if those legs were straight. The toes of his boots were worn and pointed. He smiled and flashed a mouthful of blindingly white teeth.

"Howdy," the old man offered, his eyes narrowed to slits. "You don't look much like you need a job."

"Pops," Dixie said in a scolding tone. "Be nice or wash the dishes yourself."

Pops flashed his teeth again. "This is me being nice."

"Good boy," she told him.

"Whatever happened to respecting your elders?" Pops muttered. "That's what I wanna know."

Dixie showed Wade around the kitchen and explained what he was expected to do.

The kitchen was narrow and ran the length of the establishment. A stainless-steel-lover's dream. Oven, stove top, grill on one side, several sinks and countertops and a prep area on the other. Refrigerators, freezers, dry goods, canned goods, condiments, all on the far end, near a door to the back alley.

"And for every table you bus," she told him, "I'll give you a share—a very small share, but a share—of my tips."

Wade nodded. It could be a lot of work when business was rushed, but nothing he couldn't handle. "Bus, scrape, wash, stack, take out the trash. Anything else?"

"If I think of anything, I'll let you know."

Wade blinked. She was serious. As if she hadn't already given him a full day's worth of work.

Out in the dining room, the bell over the front door dinged and more customers entered the diner.

"When can you start?" Dixie asked.

"Whenever you want me," he offered.

"Now?"

"Sure." He started rolling up his sleeves.

"Order up," Pops called.

"If you last until Lyle comes in at three to take over from you and you still want the job, we'll talk. Anything you want to ask me?"

The look on her face suggested he had overlooked something. "Such as?"

"Money?"

Wade felt like an idiot. Thousands of employees across the country had for years counted on him for a regular paycheck, hundreds of thousands of other people had their money, their retirement funds, sometimes their entire life savings, invested in Harrison Corporation, of which he'd been CEO for several years. Until his heart trouble, he'd worked his tail off making sure that neither their trust nor their money was misplaced. Harrison was profitable, its employees felt secure, its investors earned a tidy profit on their investments, because Wade and his sisters and their father, and his father, and *his* father, had done their best to see to it.

The Empire, as they jokingly referred to it in the family, had started with his great-grandfather and one small-town newspaper. Today it owned newspapers, magazines, radio and television stations, a film studio and an ad agency. Not only had Wade held it all together as more and more of the responsibility had fallen to him over the years, he'd made it all flourish. And he was damn proud of it. And he couldn't negotiate his own hourly wage at a local diner?

He wouldn't be sharing that little detail with his family.

"Yeah." He cleared his throat. "I was getting to that. What does the job pay?"

When she told him the hourly wage—before taxes, she explained—he nearly choked. He would have to work for three weeks to buy a new jock strap. So this, then, was how the rest of the world lived, he thought.

But he said nothing. Instead he nodded. "That'll be fine."

She looked at him as if she didn't quite trust him, but said, "Great. There's the dishes." She indicated three plastic tubs of dirty dishes. "Help yourself."

"In other words, get to work?" he asked with a smile.

"You read my mind."

"Order up," Pops said again.

"I'm coming." She loaded a tray, grabbed a folding stand and disappeared through the swinging door.

"Now," Pops said, putting down his spatula. He turned toward Wade and folded his arms across his scrawny chest. There was nothing scrawny, however, about the look on his face. "You may have pulled the wool over her eyes, but I've got better than twenty-twenty vision, boy. Who are you, and what are you really doing here?"

Wade paused in the middle of tying a dish towel around his waist as an apron, the way Dixie wore hers. "Pardon?" he asked to stall for time while he decided how to answer.

The old man snorted and turned back to his grill

to flip a burger. "You heard me. You're not some down-on-his-luck street bum lookin' for a job that pays peanuts." He turned to face Wade, the spatula still in his hand. "Who are you and what are you after? If you've come here to mess with the girl, you'll think you've been pulled through a knothole backward when I get through with you. I might be old, but I ain't dead yet."

"The girl? You mean Dixie?" Wade asked, incredulous. "You think I've come here to, what, mess with her? I don't even know what that means. But no, I'm just a guy looking for a job."

"Bull hockey."

Wade would have laughed at the old man's verbal expression, but the look on his face was deadly serious and nearly compelled him to blurt out the truth. It was a good thing he'd never had to face those eyes during a takeover negotiation or Wade might have buckled.

But if he told the truth, a lot of people would freak out. He chose to stick to as near the truth as possible.

"Whatever my reasons for coming here," Wade said, looking Pops straight in the eye, "they're personal. But I will tell you that I mean harm to absolutely no one, and certainly not the woman who just trusted me enough to give me a chance."

Dixie served the Mexican Platter, heavy on the jalapeños, to George Miller at table three, and a bacon cheeseburger with chili fries to Sonja Guitierez at number eight. After making the rounds with her tea pitcher, she went back to the counter.

A few minutes later she stepped into the kitchen. As she had every time during the past couple of hours, she gave a start at the sight of her new dishwasher. At least six feet of lean, gorgeous man who so obviously did not belong in her small diner kitchen, but who somehow looked just right with his sleeves rolled up and his arms plunged to the elbows in soap suds as he scrubbed one of Pop's skillets. The open collar of his shirt revealed a scar that disappeared down inside his shirt. She had a sudden urge to find out how far down that scar went.

At the thought her pulse raced and an odd tickle danced around her insides.

Whoa. Was she having a physical reaction to a man? A physical reaction of a…well, okay, just say it, of a sexual nature? Sheesh. It had been so long since she'd felt any such stirrings, she didn't know what to make of the situation.

Should she run for her life, or jump his bones?

Maybe she was coming down with a bug.

"How's it going?" she asked. *Stupid, stupid, stupid.* Why did she feel the need to speak to him, to get him to speak to her?

He shrugged. "You tell me."

Dixie blinked. Oh. He was responding to what she'd said, not what she'd thought. Thank God.

She looked around. The tubs of dirty dishes from the breakfast shift were gone. Trays of clean glasses stood stacked in their proper place alongside stacks of clean plates and a stack of napkin-wrapped cutlery settings ready for use.

"Wow," she said. "You've been busy." She hadn't expected so much work out of him so quickly.

"That's what you're paying me for," he said with a smile.

How could anyone be so damned cheerful while washing dishes? Dixie hated washing dishes. She'd hated it from the day she'd opened the diner and realized what a horrendous job it was cleaning up after so many customers all day long.

Not that she minded the customers! God love and bless each and every one of them with a hearty appetite. But that didn't mean she had to like washing their dishes. She had dirty dishes aplenty at home every day.

Out in the dining room, the bell over the front door dinged.

She turned toward the doorway. "Back to work."

The bell over the front door continued to ding frequently with the comings and goings of customers. The afternoon business was good. Wade made it out to the dining room a couple of times to bus tables, but spent the bulk of the afternoon in the kitchen elbow-deep in soapy water. He actually worked up a sweat, but he figured that was more due to the steam rising in his face than from physical exertion. He worked out regularly and was in good shape. No pile of dirty dishes could get the best of him.

When the front bell dinged again at 3:30 p.m., Dixie, who was building a salad at the counter across from the stove, heaved a sigh.

"That'll be the boys," Pops said with a smile.

Dixie looked up at the clock over the door. "Right on time." She started for the door.

Wade got a funny feeling in the pit of his stomach. *The boys.*

His boss didn't make it out of the kitchen before the swinging door shot inward and two small tornados burst into the room.

"Mom! Mom!" the oldest called in breathless excitement.

According to Wade's research, that would be ten-year-old Ben McCormick.

"I'm right here," Dixie said calmly. "No need to shout."

The boy shifted his backpack from one shoulder to the other. "Gary Thompson fell down the stairs and broke his nose. There was blood everywhere. It was way cool."

"Yeah," the younger boy agreed wholeheartedly. "Way cool."

This, Wade knew, would be Tate McCormick, age eight.

"Shame on both of you," Dixie gave them a deep frown. "Someone getting hurt is not cool."

Both boys grinned and said in unison, "Yes, ma'am."

Wade stood at his sink and stared, something deep inside him going still and soft and warm.

"Who's he?" Tate asked, pointing at him.

God, Wade thought, they were so…perfect. That was the only word he could think of, regardless of the little-boy dirt and sweat and mess that covered them, or the shirttail that was only half tucked or the shoelace that was untied. Those things were simply typical parts of typical boys. It was the big eyes—brown on one, blue on the other—the smiles, the sheer energy emanating from them, the freckles on one, the cowlick on the other, that captured him.

These were the sons of the man whose heart beat in Wade's chest. He knew it. Felt it more certainly than anything in his life.

"This is our new day-shift dishwasher," Dixie explained. "Wade Harrison, these are my sons. Ben is ten, and this is Tate."

"I'm eight," Tate rushed to clarify.

"We call him Tater," Ben announced. "'Cuz he's just a little spud. You don't look like any dishwasher I ever saw."

"I don't?" Wade asked, trying to keep up with the change of subject. "What does a dishwasher look like?"

Both boys looked at Wade with total innocence in their big brown eyes.

"Like that." Ben, the oldest, pointed at the stainless steel automatic dishwashing machine next to the sink. Then both boys giggled.

Pops chortled. "Had me going. For a minute, there, I thought they were gonna say a dishwasher was supposed to look like a girl."

"Pardon?" Wade said.

"They wouldn't dare," Dixie said with a dark glare for Pops. "He means Keesha, our previous dishwasher."

"Where'd she go, Mom?" Tate asked. "Where'd Keesha go?"

Dixie put an arm around her youngest son's shoulder. "Her husband got a new job in Dallas, so they had to move."

"I knew that," Ben said. "She left last week." He gave his brother a slight shove for emphasis. "'Member? We had to wash our own dishes that one time."

Tate made a face. "Oh, yeah. Ugh."

"You washed your own dishes?" Wade asked them.

They stuck out their chests as if about to take credit for having built the Empire State Building. "Sure did," Ben admitted.

"Yes, indeedy," Tate said with a sharp nod.

"I bet you did a good job of it, too," Wade told them.

"Yes, indeedy," Tate said again, this time with a wide grin that showed a missing upper canine.

Ben's eyes narrowed slightly. "How come you wanna know?"

"Well," Wade said, "I'm new here. I wouldn't want to get in your way or anything." He held up a wet, sudsy dishrag. "Next time you eat I'll be sure and let you do your own cleanup."

Both boys gaped, horror slowly filling their eyes. "Mom?" Tate cried.

"We don't really have to, do we?" Ben asked his mother, his voice tentative.

At the grill, Pops let out a loud cackle. "Got you good, didn't he, boys? Got you a good'n, yessiree, Bob."

Wide-eyed, Tate asked Wade, "You were kidding?"

Wade grinned. "I was kidding."

"Oh, I don't know," Dixie said with a nudge to each of her sons. "I think the idea has merit."

"Mo-om," Tate protested

"Mom, no," Ben cried. "Oh. You're kidding, too, right? Sheesh. Grown-ups."

"Maybe I was only half-kidding," Dixie said. "By the time I was your age, Ben, I was doing the dishes every day for my whole family."

"Yeah, but you're a girl."

Pops made a strangling sound and tried to look as innocent as an angel. It wasn't working.

Dixie glared first at Pops, then at the boys. "And that means…?" She propped her fists on her hips and narrowed her eyes at Ben.

"Oh, uh…" Ben hung his head, shuffled his feet and peeked up at his mother with a small grin. "Uh, gee, nothing, Mom."

"You're darn right, nothing." She nodded sharply. "Unless you're worried that you, as a mere boy, might not be able to do as good a job as a girl could."

"Aw, Mom."

"Aw, Mom," she mimicked back at him with a smile.

Wade watched the byplay, and, as trite as it sounded even to him, he felt his heart melt. And why not, he thought. It was their father's heart.

"What kind of homework do you have?" their mother asked them.

The youngest one, Tate, made a face, complete with gagging noises for sound effects. "Ugh. Yucky math."

"Poor baby." She smoothed a hand over his head and smiled.

"Huh. You think that's bad," Ben said, "I've gotta write a *paragraph*. A whole, stinkin' *paragraph*."

Dixie chuckled. "About what?"

"A subject of my choosing." He said it as though pronouncing his own death sentence.

It was all Wade could do to keep from laughing out loud. He really needed to spend more time with his nieces and nephews. He'd forgotten how much fun kids could be.

Easy for him to say, he silently admitted, since the kids in question weren't his responsibility. Whenever he needed a break he could simply send them off to their parents.

"Come on, boys," Dixie told her sons. "Take the back booth and get started on this dreaded homework. I'll bring you a snack to tide you over till dinner."

The boys started out of the kitchen, dragging their backpacks behind them.

"Pick 'em up, boys," she warned.

"Yes, ma'am," they said in unison. And they shouldered their bags.

Wade chuckled. "You have great kids."

Dixie smiled with pleasure. "Thank you. I agree."

Pop laughed. "Yeah, and they think they're pretty great, too, if you ask them."

Dixie rolled her eyes. "We have a little work to do in the humility department. They sometimes take too much after their father."

"Is that bad?" Wade asked, glad that his voice sounded only slightly curious. As though he was simply making conversation. Not as though his breath hung on her response.

She chuckled. "Sometimes it is."

Wade bit his tongue to keep from asking her to explain.

Dixie took a couple of apples and glasses of milk to her sons and checked on the progress of their homework. "Here you go. How's it coming?"

Both boys groaned and rolled their eyes.

"I don't get nines," Tate complained.

"What's not to get?" Ben said. "It's one less than ten."

"Oh. Huh?"

"What I don't get is what I'm supposed to write about," Ben griped. He'd written his name at the top of his notebook page, but nothing else.

Dixie set down their apples and milk. "Stop and eat. Maybe something will come to you. What about Little League?" she suggested.

"What about it? The game's not till Thursday."

"You could write about why you like to play."

"Hey, cool! Thanks, Mom. Why I Like Baseball, by Benjamin McCormick. I like it."

"Me, too," she agreed.

"Mom." Tate pushed his math away and picked up his apple.

"Yes?"

He rubbed his apple against his shirt and inspected the shine. "I like Wade."

"You do, huh?"

He took a giant, juicy bite of apple and nodded yes.

"Think I should hire him?"

"I thought you already did," Ben said.

"Just trying him out for now," she told them. "See how he does."

"Gol', Mom, it's only dishwashing," Ben told her. "What's the big deal? Who can't wash dishes?"

"Me," Tate piped up. "I'm allergic."

Ben's "You wish," was accompanied by a snort, and the swing of his foot under the table, directly into Tate's leg.

Tate's response was to grin and kick back. Dixie didn't need to look beneath the table to know the latter. She knew her boys. That was enough. That and their body language, the slight lean to one side, the little bounce when the foot connected with the opponent's shin. So predictable, her boys were. Usually, anyway.

"When you're finished eating, take your dishes to the kitchen," she told them. They knew the routine, but it never hurt to remind them.

"Yes, ma'am," they said together, both with their mouths full.

Dixie rolled her eyes and turned away. Behind the counter she picked up a full pitcher of iced tea and made another round of the room offering refills.

She would offer Wade the job. There was no reason to dilly-dally around about it.

Dixie was used to making decisions of all shapes and sizes. There was no sense in fretting over things. She weighed the pros and cons of a matter, then made her choice and lived with the consequences. Those consequences weren't always what she might wish, but they were hers, and she would make do.

At four, Earline, her evening manager, came in. Within five minutes the rest of the night crew— MaryLou, Frank and Lyle—showed up.

Dixie went to the kitchen and introduced Wade to

everyone as Lyle was taking over Wade's spot at the sink for the day.

"You're the new guy, huh?" Lyle asked.

Wade looked to Dixie with a raised brow.

"Yes," she said. "Not that I think you need it, but if you want the job, it's yours."

Wade's smile came slow and full. "Thanks. Yes. I want the job."

The relief she felt was because the job was now filled. Not, surely not, because this particular man filled it.

And that was the last thought she was going to give the man and the subject until tomorrow. So there.

"Fine," she said to her new dishwasher. She stepped out of the kitchen and retrieved a form from the shelf beneath the cash-register. "Fill this out and bring it back tomorrow. Be here at six in the morning."

"Yes, ma'am." His polite smile had just enough of a touch of the shark in it that, if she let it, might make her nervous.

But men, as a rule, did not make Dixie McCormick nervous. She'd been in love, been married, then divorced. In the bargain, she'd been blessed with the two true loves of her life—Ben and Tater. And heaven help her, two males were enough for any sane woman. Certainly her ex had never made her nervous. How could he, when she'd known him all her life? Best friends didn't make each other nervous.

At 4:30 p.m. she turned the café over to Earline, then gathered those loves of her life up and headed out, they on their bicycles, she in her car, for the five-block trip home. She put her new dishwasher and the funny feelings he generated inside her completely out of her mind. Several times.

Chapter Two

Wade followed his new boss and her sons out the door at 4:30 that afternoon and drove back to his motel, three blocks from the diner, in a daze. He had yet to stop grinning when, several moments later, he called home.

"I found them."

His father put him on the speakerphone. It was his mother who responded to Wade's remark. "Honestly, Wade, you can't simply traipse off to the wilds of Texas—"

Wade broke out laughing. "You say that like it's the middle of the Sahara Desert." He could almost see one of her fiercest frowns; his mother was a champion frowner.

"It might as well be," she complained. "Texas, for God's sake."

"Texas has been very good to us," he reminded her. "We have two productive printing plants in Fort Worth and a profitable shopping mall in Houston."

"That doesn't mean I want my only son there," his mother said tersely. "You know it hasn't been that long since—"

"Mother," he interrupted. "It's been two years since my transplant, I'm in excellent health, my doctor says there's no problem with my taking a trip and I'm here. It's a done deal."

"I'm sure if I knew how you discovered the name of your donor, I would not approve. Neither would the medical community."

"Relax." If he'd been in the room with her, he'd have dropped a light kiss on his mother's forehead. Instead, he chuckled. "I did nothing illegal. Mostly it involved reading the paper and looking at a few police reports. Public records."

"You know who your donor was." His father wasn't about to let Wade make his case without his input. "Why did you need to go to Texas at all?"

"I need to know more than just his name. I need to know what kind of man he was."

"I don't see why," his mother said tersely. "What are you going to do if you find out he was…unsavory?"

Wade and his father burst out laughing. Either of them would have used a harsher word, but Myrna Harrison did not, would not, under threat of death, allow anything approaching a swear word to pass her lips.

Wade grinned. "Maybe I'll start being unsavory, too, and blame it on him."

His mother tsked. "This is about that comment you made when you woke up from surgery."

"Two points for Mother," he said.

"There's no need for sarcasm. I thought we decided months ago that your comment about 'the boys' meant nothing."

"You decided," he said. "I met them."

"Met who?" his mother demanded. "The boys?"

"Yes." He still felt the sense of awe swelling in his chest, just like when he'd first seen them in the diner's kitchen.

"Wade, no," his mother protested. "You didn't go up to those boys and tell them who you are."

"Would you give me a little credit? As far as they're concerned, I'm just the new dishwasher."

"The what?" His father's voice, finally.

"That's my other news. I took a job today."

A long silence stretched from New York to Texas and back again. Then suddenly both of his parents spoke at once.

"A what?"

"Washing dishes? You don't know how to wash dishes."

"Hush, Myrna," his father said. "Son, explain yourself."

He told them how he came to be working for the mother of the boys he'd come to find.

"Well, for heaven's sake," his mother said. "When can we expect you home?"

"Home?" The question gave Wade a jolt, and it shouldn't have. That told him how affected he was by meeting Ben and Tate McCormick. He hadn't even thought of going home. He'd thought of nothing but the boys since he'd entered the diner and saw their mother.

Well, okay, he'd thought of other things, too. A pair of deep blue eyes—Dixie's. And dishpan hands—his.

"Yes," his mother said. "You remember home, don't you? New York? That place where you live?"

"Very funny," he responded. "But don't leave the light on for me. I'm going to spend some time here, check things out."

"Things?" his father asked. "You've seen the boys in question. I assume they were fine. Case closed."

"They seem fine, yes." Wade felt inexplicable anger at the thought of leaving Tribute and returning to New York. The feeling wasn't rational, he knew, but it was there. "I just want to stick around long enough to make sure. Besides, I don't want to walk out on the diner, on my job, without giving some notice."

"A pitiful excuse," his mother said in the same

tone she might have used when asking if that was a skunk she was smelling. "What dishwasher ever gave notice when quitting?"

"This one," Wade said. "Relax, Mom. Remember that last birthday I had? It was my thirty-sixth. I'm a big boy. I know how to think for myself." He hoped his smile came through in his voice. He wouldn't hurt his mother's feelings for the world. Even when she did try to treat him like a kid.

"You never told us what the boys are like," his father reminded him.

"I don't know," he said, hedging, not sure what to say. "I only saw them for a couple of minutes."

"You," his father said, "who once deduced that the Carrington chain of movie theaters would be a bad investment after three minutes with the CEO, and you cannot tell what two young boys are like?"

"I didn't have several million dollars riding on what I thought of them. They seemed like good kids, smart, funny. You know—kids," Wade responded. "I know next to nothing about kids."

"But you know they're healthy?"

"They appear to be."

"They're clothed, have plenty to eat, go to school?"

Wade sighed. "Yes."

"Then, I would say your mission has been accomplished." As head of the family and the corporation, Jeffery Harrison was used to being obeyed. It came through in his voice when he added, "So you can come home now with a clear mind."

"The last I heard," Wade said, "the company was doing great in the capable hands of my sisters. I'm not needed at home."

"You're not needed in Texas, either," his mother said sharply.

"Oh, I don't know about that," Wade said easily, despite the tension starting to tighten his gut. "I'm needed to wash dishes at Dixie's Diner."

"Wade—"

"Look." He cut off his mother. "I'm fine, I've got all my meds with me. Tell yourselves I've gone on a much-needed vacation if that helps. I'm going to hang around here for a while." He wouldn't ask if that was all right with them, because it was his decision, not theirs.

It was silent for a long moment, then his mother sighed heavily. "I'm sure dinner is almost ready, so we'll let you go. For now," she added darkly.

"I love you, Mother. You, too, Dad. Give my love to the girls," he added.

After a couple more rounds of "love you" and "miss you" and "call soon," they finally ended the call.

Wade fell back onto the bed in his motel room with a groan. He loved his family, but, Lord, they could drive him nuts. Especially since his surgery. He understood that they were still frightened for him, worried about him, and probably always would be.

He'd been within hours of dying the night of his heart transplant.

This was the first time he'd been away from home since then. They couldn't fuss over him. Couldn't take care of him. Couldn't watch him take his pills. Couldn't nag him about exercising. "Do it, but don't overdo it."

He was gathering the energy to sit up when his stomach growled.

He laughed. He'd been in a diner all day and hadn't eaten. Now he had to find himself a meal. There were several other places to eat along the mile-long stretch of Main Street; he'd noticed them when he drove in to town that morning. He would walk. He needed the exercise.

Part of his medication consisted of a steroid that helped prevent his body from rejecting the new heart, but it also, among other things, softened his bones. To combat that, he spent a portion of every day doing weight-bearing exercises. Everything from walking to running to weight lifting. If he was to stay in Tribute for more than a few days, he would need to find a way to work out with weights.

Wade had imagined that the days in Texas would be warm, and this one was. Being more than a hundred miles from the gulf, he'd figured that the air would be on the dry side. On that he'd been mistaken. By the time he walked to the end of Main and crossed the street to return on the other side, his shirt was sticking to his back.

On his way he passed a flower-and-gift shop, grocery store, ice cream shop, auto parts store, and dentist's office. Next to the pizza parlor sat a bank, then the town square. He didn't walk the square, but noticed the businesses lining it included a newspaper office. It was still open, so he decided that after he ate, if they were closed, he would walk by and peer through the front windows. Harrison Corporation owned more than a few newspapers.

His great-grandfather had started the family's first newspaper from nothing, wrote the columns, edited, set the type, printed the copies and sold them. A true one-man operation for the first several months of publication. But, since his had been the only paper in the tiny Wyoming town, it had been a hit.

The rest, as they said—at least, in his family—was history.

Wade would enjoy poking around this particular weekly paper, but he would settle for a view through the window later.

The center of the town square was occupied by city hall, the police station and county sheriff's office, and the courthouse. Around the perimeter sat the town library and several other small businesses.

He walked on past the square, past a ladies clothing shop, Mexican restaurant, hot dog drive-in. There was a video rental store, a feed-and-seed store, post office, hamburger place, real estate office, law firm, doctor's office, Dixie's Diner, hardware store, two other motels, four bars, three gas stations, plus a gas station with a convenience store and an attached car wash.

Down a side street here and there he spotted a fire station, an auto repair shop, veterinarian clinic, VFW hall, several churches and a small apartment building.

Eventually he quit taking note of the businesses and simply walked. It felt good to be out in the open, to be moving. To be breathing and feel the heart beating beneath his sternum. Never again would he take such a miracle as a heartbeat for granted. He walked until he reached his motel again, then kept walking until he returned to the Mexican restaurant. The aromas coming from their doorway lured him in.

As he ate the enchiladas covered in salsa hot enough to clean out his sinuses, he thought of the paperwork he had yet to fill out for Dixie McCormick, and smiled. He couldn't remember the last time he'd had to fill out an employment form, but it might have been when he was sixteen.

It was over a mouthful of refried beans that he realized that out there on the main street of the Texas town of Tribute there was one—count 'em, *one*—traffic light.

He'd heard about towns this small, maybe even driven through one without realizing it, but he didn't think he'd ever stayed in one.

Who would have thought that Wade Harrison had led a sheltered life?

* * *

Dixie didn't have time to wonder whether or not her new dishwasher would remember to fill out his paperwork and bring it with him in the morning. She would be pleased enough if he showed up.

She would be even more pleased if somebody would give her about three extra hours every day. With three more hours on this day, she might get the house a little cleaner, read a chapter or two on the novel she started a month ago, indulge in a long, hot soak in the tub and possibly even get to bed in time to allow for eight hours of sleep.

As things stood, she felt as if she'd done pretty good getting the yard mowed—with "help" from the boys. She oversaw the rest of the boys' homework, ran their Little League uniforms through the laundry, cooked dinner, supervised the cleanup, watched a half hour of television with the boys, then sent them one at a time to their baths, then bed.

"G'night, Mom."

She leaned over and kissed Ben good-night. "'Night, Ben." She moved to the other twin bed across the room and kissed Tate. "'Night, Tater. Love you both."

"Love you, too, Mom," they said together.

Dixie's heart swelled. No matter how exhausted she got, hearing her sons say they loved her filled her with so much joy it sometimes felt impossible to hold it all in.

Benny and Tater love me.

I love Benny and Tater.

Life simply didn't get any better, she thought.

Oh, a little more money would be nice. Okay, a lot more money, so her boys could go to college. She was socking a little away every month, praying that the stock market and mutual fund gods would be kind.

A man would—naw, scratch that. She'd had a man in her life, God rest his soul. Jimmy Don had been her high school heartthrob. A good-time, barrel-of-laughs kind of guy. Too bad he never grew up. She didn't want another child to raise. She was just fine on her own.

There was one man she wondered about, though—her new dishwasher, Wade Harrison. He didn't fit. If he was an unemployed drifter, it was only because he wanted to be. And she'd bet her most comfortable shoes that his situation, if it was even real, was temporary. He reeked of money, wealth with a capital W. Polished. Privileged.

So, what, she wondered for the hundredth time, was he doing washing dishes in her diner?

She decided she didn't care. As long as he showed up and did the job, she'd be satisfied.

Wade couldn't recall the last time he'd been up and out the door before sunup. He'd forgotten how early 6:00 a.m. could be.

He decided to walk to the diner. Driving such a short distance and taking up a parking space all day when there weren't that many of them in the middle of town to begin with seemed ridiculous.

At 6:00 a.m. sharp he entered Dixie's Diner right behind Pops. Dixie and her boys were already there.

Wade was surprised to see young Ben and Tate McCormick at the diner so early. Dixie had put them at a booth in the banquet room this time. There was a television mounted on the wall in there, currently tuned to cartoons.

"You came back," Pops said to Wade.

"I work here," Wade answered with a slight shrug.

Pops looked at him and smiled. "Yep, guess you do, at that."

"You came," Dixie said.

Wade couldn't tell if that was surprise or relief in her voice. "Was I not supposed to?"

"No," she said quickly. "I mean, yes. You were supposed to." She finally smiled. "I just wasn't sure you would."

"With my paperwork all complete." He handed her the finished form.

She glanced at it and frowned. "Your address is Main Street?"

He shrugged. "The Tribute Inn until I find a place." As soon as he said the words, he realized he was going to do just that—find a place to live. An apartment, maybe a small house to rent.

He hadn't come to Tribute to stay, but he wouldn't leave until he had alleviated his concerns about Ben and Tate. There was no law that said he couldn't be comfortable in the meantime.

"Where did you live before the Tribute Inn?" Dixie asked him.

"New York." He wasn't going to lie. Unless he had to.

"Oh, yeah," she said while reading the form. A moment later she looked up and smiled. "Well, thanks for taking care of this. Now I need you to roll some more silverware in paper napkins."

"No problem."

"And please check the salt and pepper shakers at all the tables. Lyle's got a sick mare at home and hasn't been getting much sleep lately. Sometimes he misses a table or two at closing."

"I'll check them."

"Thanks." Dixie smiled and thought he was surely too good to be true. An agreeable man who didn't mind having a woman question him and tell him what to do, even if it was the lowliest of jobs? What manner of strange creature was this?

With Wade handling those chores, Dixie turned to start the coffee before customers arrived, but Pops was already on it. That meant there was nothing standing between her and the paperwork from the night before. Dammit.

"Do your boys always come to work with you in the mornings?"

She turned back toward Wade. "What? Oh, yes.

I don't want to leave them at home alone when I come to work."

"Oh," Wade said. "I don't blame you. I guess school isn't far from here?"

"It's just a few blocks," she told him.

Wade took a breath and plunged into the subject he'd been wanting to raise. "What about their father?"

"He died a couple of years ago."

"Oh. I'm sorry."

"Thanks, but we were divorced. He was out of the picture for a long time before then."

"That's rough."

She gave a short chuckle. "Not nearly as rough as keeping him around would have been, God rest his soul."

"Oh." He looked blank for a moment.

"Sorry," she said with a grimace. "I don't talk much about him." And she wondered why she was running off at the mouth this time. "The boys barely remember him."

"That's too bad," Wade offered. "I can't imagine growing up without a father, but these days I guess kids do it all the time."

"They do," she agreed. "And many of them are better off for it. I know mine are."

There came that blank look on Wade's face again. "I'll just go check those salt and pepper shakers," he said. "Then I'll get to the silverware."

"Thanks." She wondered what Wade was thinking to give him that blank look.

Wade was thinking that maybe McCormick hadn't been the best father, but he wanted Jimmy Don remembered in a better light, not for what he hadn't done right or well, but for that one great thing he did do that made such a difference to so many people.

He needed a plan.

During the next couple of days, business at Dixie's Diner kept everybody hopping. Wade felt the beginnings of a friendship developing between Pops and himself. The old man knew a little, or sometimes a lot, about practically everything—particularly if it had to do with Tribute or Texas or horses—and he was full of stories that generally started with, "Back when I was a boy," and ended with, "And you can take that to the bank."

Wade even felt as if Ben and Tate were beginning to accept him, if not as a friend, exactly, then at least as part of the diner. He found himself eager each morning to see them and watching the clock every afternoon, waiting for the minute they barreled through the front door to announce all the news from school and complain about their homework.

"Fourteen ninety-two," Ben muttered at their morning table in the banquet room. "Fourteen ninety-two. How am I supposed to know what the heck happened way back then?"

Wade brought orange juice for the boys while Dixie ran the electronic cash register through its morning paces to get it up and running.

"Way back when?" he asked.

Ben grimaced. "Fourteen ninety-two."

"Columbus," Wade prompted.

"What about him? Is that when he discovered America?" Ben groaned and buried his face in his hands. "How am I supposed to keep it all straight in my head?"

"It's a poem," Wade offered.

"What's a poem?"

"'In 1492, Columbus sailed the ocean blue.' Or something like that. That's how I always remember it."

"No foolin'?" Tate asked.

"No kidding?" Ben asked.

"No foolin', no kidding."

"Gol', thanks, Wade," Ben said. "What else do you know?"

Wade laughed. "Sorry. That's about it."

He smiled all the way back to the kitchen. God, those boys were something. Seeing them made his day.

But oddly it was their mother who filled his thoughts the most. He didn't know whether to be irritated or intrigued by her. She worked too damn hard. He had the strongest urge to carry her away to somewhere soft and quiet and massage her tired feet until she purred.

Every time that picture floated through his little

pea-size brain, the next image was of her whacking him up the side of his head with a plastic-coated menu for being too fresh and presumptuous.

But with her customers she was always laughing or encouraging or commiserating or whatever that particular customer needed. She considered them all her friends.

Every evening Wade walked. After a few days he knew the town front to back, side to side. It was a nice little town—clean, with new school buildings, rodeo grounds, a small hospital, a community swimming pool next to a park. On the other side of town sat another park, this one with three baseball fields with backstops. One field came complete with two six-tier bleachers and a couple of all-purpose concession stands. Pretty fancy stuff for such a small town.

Thursday evening Wade was three blocks away from the park on the south side of town when he heard shouts and cheers. When he drew near and rounded the last corner and the park came into view, he realized it was a ball game.

The first thing Wade realized was that the town of Tribute was so quiet and peaceful that a man could hear a softball game from three blocks away. The second thing he realized was that this was a Little League game. He recognized Ben McCormick as the second baseman.

And someone recognized him. "Hey, Wade!" Tate McCormick waved from beneath the stands, where he played with a group of boys his age. "Guys, it's Wade!"

"Hey, Tate." Wade tucked his hands into the front pockets of his jeans and ambled over toward the back side of the stands. "What are you guys up to?"

"Chasing a lizard," Tate stated proudly.

"No fooling? Is it a big one?"

"Nah," another kid said.

"He's just a little 'zard," Tate said. "Did ya come to watch Ben play?"

"I guess so," Wade said, stepping back when Tate crawled out from beneath the bleachers. "I was out taking a walk and heard all the yelling. Thought I'd see what was going on."

"They're playing the Wildcats from Bremond."

"Are these Wildcats any good?" Wade asked.

Tate pinched his nose and made a face. "Wildcats *stink*."

"Yeah? Who's winning?"

Tate threw out his arms and shrugged. "I dunno. Haven't been watching. Let's go ask Mom." Without waiting, he grabbed Wade's hand and started around the bleachers and up into them. The next thing Wade knew, he was seated between Dixie and Tate on the fourth row up. Pops sat on Dixie's other side.

"Out taking in the local color?" Dixie asked with a smile.

"I went for a walk and wondered what all the yelling was about," Wade said.

Tate leaned around him and grinned at his mother. "And I brought him up here so he could watch the game. What's the score?"

"Six to four," Dixie supplied.

"We're six?" Tate asked, his face scrunched up as if he wasn't sure he was going to like her answer.

"We're six," she told him.

"All right!" Tate made a fist and pumped his arm in the air. "I told ya, the Wildcats stink."

"Yes," Wade said seriously. "You told me."

"Hey, Pops, we had a lizard down under the stands," Tate called out. "Mom, can I have a soda?"

"Do you have any money?" Dixie asked.

"No."

"I guess that answers your question, then, doesn't it?"

"Aw, Mom. Okay, I got enough for a soda."

"You do, huh?" Dixie said. "Well, if you want to spend it on a drink, that's up to you. But there won't be any more money coming your way until Monday."

"None?" Tate cried, just on the verge of outrage.

Following the conversation, Wade felt as if he was at a tennis match, back and forth.

"Not a penny, and you still have to buy your lunch tomorrow."

"Tightwad," Pops muttered to Dixie. "If you're

gonna go," he said louder to Tate, "get me a root beer. Keep the change." He winked and handed the boy a five.

"Pops," Dixie said darkly.

Pops blinked in exaggerated innocence. "What?"

Wade copied Pops and pulled a five from his pocket and handed it to Tate. "I'll have whatever you're having."

"I changed my mind." Tate grinned. "I'm having what he's having." He pointed at Pops.

"Watch it, Bub." Dixie gave him a mock glare and raised her fist toward him.

Tate grinned. "It was worth a try. You want something?"

Dixie leaned over and ruffled his hair. "I want a kiss, but since we're in public, I'll settle for whatever you and Wade are having."

In the process of releasing Tate and lowering her arm to her side again, the back of her forearm brushed against Wade's arm. A spark, sharp and hot, arced between them.

Dixie sucked in air between her teeth.

Wade inhaled sharply.

She looked at him, startled.

He looked at her, stunned.

"Yeah?" Tate said. "Then gimmie a fiver."

The sound of the boy's voice reached down into the deep recesses of Wade's brain and brought him back to awareness. He swallowed, hard, his mouth lined with cotton.

Dixie seemed to be having as much trouble as he was. "Five?" she finally said, her gaze still locked on Wade. "A soda doesn't cost that much."

"No," Tate said with a snicker, "but you know how those delivery charges are. They just keep going up and up."

Dixie finally looked away, and Wade felt suddenly new and exposed, as if she'd taken a layer of his skin with her.

"Highway robbery," Dixie said to Tate, handing him a five from the purse in her lap. Her hand was shaking.

Good, Wade thought. At least he wasn't the only one who felt as if lightning had just struck.

Wade watched her watch her youngest son traipse down the steps until the boy reached the ground and dashed the five yards to the concession stand. She seemed to have recovered faster and easier than he was able to.

He cleared his throat. "He's really something," Wade told her. "Both your boys are. You must be proud."

She looked dazed, and he wanted to grin. Hell, he wanted to shout. *Dixie McCormick is not indifferent to me!*

And he, it appeared, was not indifferent to her.

Of course, he'd known the latter. Every time she came into the kitchen, his gaze was drawn to her like steel filings to a magnet. He nearly groaned at the thought. He'd become a cliché. Then he smiled, realizing he didn't care, because what little he knew about Dixie he liked. And he liked being attracted to her. And he liked that she'd felt that shocking, electrifying touch every bit as much as he had.

"Of course I'm proud," she answered. "As a peacock. But that's not what you were thinking about just now."

He let out a laugh. "Are you a mind reader?"

She laughed, but a telltale blush colored her cheeks. "No."

Okay, time to move things along a notch. "Actually, I was having a nice little fantasy about you and me under the bleachers, alone, in the dark." The instant the words were out, Wade wanted them back.

She stared at him, stunned, her blush turning even deeper. Then she glanced sharply away. "Oh, look." She motioned toward the ball field in a none-too-subtle change of subject. "Third out. Our guys are up to bat now. And here comes Tater with our drinks."

"Got it," Wade said quietly. He didn't need it spelled out for him to get the message. It had been a long, long time since he had blundered so badly with a woman. Now it was his turn to blush. "Sorry. I shouldn't have said that. I was out of line."

"Forget it," she said, reaching to take the drink from the cardboard tray Tate carried.

* * *

For the rest of the game Wade and Dixie kept their attention focused on the field, yet each was more aware of the other with every passing minute.

Wade tried to distract himself by looking around at the spectators. He recognized three people as customers from the diner. Another was the assistant manager at his motel. The woman down on the first row, he thought, was a checker at the grocery store.

He glanced beyond the stands, just past the concession stand, and did a double take. "An ambulance?"

"That's *the* ambulance," Dixie told him.

"Do these Little League games get that rowdy?"

She laughed. "Not usually, no. But the EMS guys like to get out in the community whenever they can. Anytime we have a gathering of any size, you'll usually find them nearby."

Wade couldn't fathom an ambulance and crew having nothing better to do than hang around Little League games. If the rest of the world heard about this, everyone would want to live here, then the place would be as busy and hazardous as New York or any other large city.

He would just keep his mouth shut about how safe and quiet it was in Tribute, Texas.

Besides, no one he knew would believe him.

When Ben came up to bat, he popped two flies, then hit a double to left field, sending the runner at third on into home, scoring a point for his team.

"Way to go, Ben!" Tate called.

Dixie stood and yelled, "Yea, Ben!"

"Atta boy, Ben!" Wade hollered.

"Taught the kid everything he knows," Pops declared.

Dixie arched her brow and gave Pops a mock glare. "I beg your pardon?"

"About horses," Pops finished with a wrinkled grin. "Taught him everything he knows about horses. He learned his baseball from you, Dixie girl, and a damn fine job you did with him, too."

Dixie nodded her head once, sharply. "That's better."

The next batter knocked Ben in. Two more innings, and Ben's team took the Wildcats for a final score of nine to six.

"Hooray!" Tate started down the bleachers. "Dairy Queen, here we come!"

"Dairy Queen?" Wade asked Dixie as she and Pops rose and started toward the aisle.

"The parents always treat the players to ice cream after a game." she told him. "Why don't you come with us?"

Wade smiled. "I wouldn't want to intrude."

Dixie returned his smile. "Of course you would. Come on. I'll buy you a cone."

"There's a lesson here, boy," Pops told him. "When the boss wants to pay, say yes."

"Sounds like good advice to me," Wade allowed.

* * *

Dixie didn't know what to think of Wade. If she had felt that mutual zap of heat and electricity with any other man she knew, he'd have pounced on her like a duck on a june bug.

But not Wade. Thank God. He'd let her know with a look that he'd felt the same thing she'd felt, but that he wasn't going to act on it. Not yet, at least.

Then again, perhaps rather than wonder at his reaction, she should be wondering why she had reacted to him when she hadn't felt anything physical for any man in months. Maybe longer.

"Mom?"

Dixie blinked and realized Ben had been holding out his hand, waiting for her to give him the money for an ice cream cone.

"Oh. Sorry. Here. Get enough for all of us."

"We all get vanilla," Ben said to Wade. "Is that all right with you?"

"Sounds good," Wade told him.

Ben grinned and did a little skip-hop step on his way to the order window.

"He's glad you came with us," Dixie told Wade.

Wade smiled and looked around the Dairy Queen parking lot at the kids and their families, all talking at once, reliving the game, laughing, joking. He tucked his hands into his hip pockets and rocked back on his heels. "I'm glad to be here."

Dixie shook her head, tilted it and narrowed her gaze at him. "Who are you, Wade Harrison?"

He laughed. "Pardon?"

She shook her head again. "It's a cliché, I know, but, what is a man like you doing in a place like this?"

His smile slipped a notch. "You invited me to come for ice cream. But I see that this is a family thing." He motioned to all the families around them. "I appreciate the invitation, but—"

"No," she said quickly. "I didn't mean it that way. You're welcome here. I invited you because we—Pops, the boys and I—wanted you to come. We enjoy your company."

"Thank you," he said. "The feeling is mutual."

Hmm. Dixie folded her arms across her chest. "You don't strike me as a man who needs reassurance or ego stroking. Are you pulling my leg?"

"Not at all." He was the picture of innocence.

"Hmm."

"You asked what I was doing here," he said. "I took that to mean that you thought I shouldn't be here."

She shook her head. "I just wonder why you would choose to hang out in Tribute, when you could be back in New York."

A car full of teenagers drove by, the bass from the car stereo pounding a beat through the pavement, shrieks of laughter streaming from the open windows.

"Have you ever been to New York?" Wade asked her.

"I can't say that I've ever had the pleasure."

"It is a pleasure," he told her. "For some people. For others, a small town like Tribute is paradise."

"And for you?" she asked.

"Me? I like them both. But right now, Tribute is nudging out New York."

"Why?"

He met her gaze squarely and smiled. "I'm liking the view."

Good grief. She was thirty-one years old and was blushing over a man. For the second time in one night.

Heaven help her.

Chapter Three

While the McCormick family gathered around the table for Sunday dinner, the morning's rain moved east and the sun came out. Dixie managed to keep the boys in their seats long enough to finish eating, but the instant she gave the nod, she could have sworn their legs were spring loaded. They leaped from their chairs and flew out the back door. A moment later the basketball made a *splat, splat, splat* against the wet driveway.

Dixie let out a sigh. "I know I used to have that much energy sometime in my past, but I sure don't remember it."

"Old age settin' in?" Pops asked, his tongue plainly in his cheek.

He knew just the right buttons to push. Her back straightened as if she'd taken a hit with a cattle prod. "Bite your tongue."

Pops chuckled. "What you need, little girl, is a vacation."

"Yeah, like *that's* going to happen." She pushed herself up from the table and moved to the counter. "Pie?"

"Did I cook it?" he asked.

"Of course. It's apple."

"Then I'll take a slice. You know, if you were to find yourself interested in some fella, that'd be just fine with me."

Dixie nearly dropped the knife she was using to slice the pie. *"What?"*

"Don't 'what' me," he responded with a laugh. "I saw the way you and that new dishwasher looked at each other the other night after Ben's game. And every day at work since then."

Dixie's heart jumped up to her throat and her face heated up. "That new dishwasher has a name, Pops."

"Yeah. It's Wade. And don't change the subject, little girl. Pretty woman like you needs to have a love life. Let's face it, you ain't gettin' any younger."

"Now *you're* calling me old?"

"You're still sidestepping the subject."

"Which is?"

"You—on a date—with a man."

"I've had dates," she protested.

"Not lately. Not this year, nor most of last."

"What do you do, take notes?"

Pops heaved a sigh. "All I'm saying is, Jimmy Don was my grandson, and I loved him. You loved him, even after the divorce, and I know you had to divorce him or go crazy. He couldn't be bothered with growing up, and you had two babies. You didn't need a third. But he's been gone a long time now, and all men aren't irresponsible idiots. You need a man, and your boys need a father."

"Pops!" She was stunned. He'd never talked about Jimmy Don this way, never interfered in her life in such a personal way before.

They had spoken of the needs of her sons in the past, though. Their need for a male role model. At Pops's age, it wasn't fair to expect him to fill that role, but he was all she had in that respect.

Her father was a wonderful grandfather, but he and Dixie's mother lived in Florida and saw the boys only a couple of times a year. Their other grandfather, Hal—Pops' son, Jimmy Don's dad, and Dixie's ex-father-in-law—filled the void when he could, but he was a long-haul trucker, gone for weeks at a time and home only a day or two before heading out again.

That left Pops, who had always insisted he wanted to be in their lives on a daily basis.

"The boys have you," she told him. "They're

blessed to have you, and they love you dearly. And what makes you think I want anything to do with a man? When would I have time, for crying out loud?"

"If you're not gonna cut that pie, just bring it on over here and I'll slice my own piece."

"Have at it." She flopped the entire pie down in front of him. "A man in my life, indeed."

"And why not?" He sliced through the pie until it was all sectioned off, then lifted a piece onto his plate. "Any ice cream?"

Dixie pursed her lips and rolled her eyes.

"I'll get it." Pops pushed himself from his chair and ambled over to the fridge. He pulled a half gallon of vanilla ice cream from the freezer and set it on the counter. Before dishing out a scoop, he nuked his slice of pie. The sweet scent of apples and cinnamon filled the air. By the time Pops returned to the table, the pie was steaming and the ice cream was melting around the edges.

"Now that," he said with satisfaction, "is one good dessert. And you, Dixie-doodle, are one heck of a woman who deserves a good man."

"Why?" she asked. "What did I do wrong?"

"Ha! Smart mouth." He forked pie and ice cream into his mouth. "I'm just sayin', if you and New York Boy wanna make cow eyes at each other, it's fine by me, that's all."

Dixie helped herself to a slice of pie. "Well, now that I have your approval, I'll just go jump his bones."

"Might be good for you," he muttered.

"Pops!"

While Dixie and Pops shared pie à la mode, Wade moved the meager belongings he'd brought with him to Texas into a tiny, two-room apartment. The smell of fresh paint permeated the air inside. The apartment was furnished with secondhand furniture, but it was well kept and clean.

Moving in meant parking his rental car in the single slot out front and carrying in his suitcase.

But he had a kitchen now, such as it was. After he put away the items in his suitcase, he drove to the grocery on Main and stocked up on a few basics, along with a bag of his biggest weakness—butterscotch candy.

That evening he stretched out on his sofa with his laptop and caught up on nonbusiness e-mail. He'd traded daily maid service for more space and considered it a good deal.

After logging off his computer, he looked up at the water-stained ceiling above him and smiled. His mother would have a coronary, his father would disapprove and his sisters would be amused.

During the following week, Dixie came to understand how a bug under a microscope must feel. Every time she and Wade were in the same room, she could feel his gaze on her like a touch. Sometimes soft, sometimes hot. Sometimes his eyes were laughing. She couldn't help but look back. He had a way of keeping her off balance that at first irritated her, then puzzled her, then intrigued her. As recently as last month she'd still been referred to as Jimmy Don's girl. It felt strange for another man to pay attention to her.

But the two of them were not in a cocoon. The diner was full of people. The first of them being Pops. Her late-ex-husband's grandfather watched the byplay between her and Wade as though it was a show put on for his amusement. He seemed to particularly enjoy her confusion. The rat.

Naturally Ben and Tate eventually clued in that something was going on between and among the grown-ups in their lives, but grown-ups were weird, everybody knew that, so they didn't let it worry them.

"Dixie? Are you okay?"

"What?" Dixie gave a start and nearly dumped a BLT and fries into Carrie Miller's lap. "Oh. Sorry. No. Yes. Fine."

Carrie laughed. "Come again?"

Dixie joined her and laughed at herself. She placed the order down carefully in front of Carrie. "I'm sorry," she offered. "My mind was wandering."

"Maybe to that new dishwasher you hired last week?"

If anyone so much as breathed on her, Dixie would have fallen over.

"Cat got your tongue?"

Dixie had known Carrie since first grade, yet suddenly she didn't know what to say to her.

"Yoo-hoo." Carrie waved her hand in front of Dixie's eyes. "Earth to Dixie."

"I guess she's out to lunch," Dixie said with a laugh. "I'm sorry. What did you ask?"

"I'm not sure I remember."

Just then Wade came out of the kitchen. With an empty tub on his hip, he bussed the booth that was two down from Carrie's.

"Ah," Carrie said. "Now I remember."

"Well, you can forget it," Dixie said darkly.

She left Carrie to her BLT and went back to deliver two more orders. Wade was back in the kitchen by the time she returned to top off Carrie's iced tea.

"Besides," Dixie told her with a hiss, "I barely know the man."

"He was checking you out like a man who wanted to get to know you a whole lot better."

"Oh, he was not."

"He was," Carrie insisted.

"Was he? Really?" She hadn't been imagining it?

"Yes, really. Are you going to go for it?" Carrie wanted to know.

"Go for— Of course not."

"Liar, liar, pants on fire."

"I was going to offer you a piece of pie, on the house."

"What kind?"

"Forget it," Dixie said. "I don't give freebies to people who call me a liar."

"So, you're not hot for the dishwasher?"

"Of course not," Dixie protested. "Don't be ridiculous."

Carrie grinned. Evilly. "Methinks thou doth protest too much."

"Methinks your imagination is running away in that little pea brain of yours, girlfriend."

Carrie sighed heavily. "I give up. For now. But, girlfriend, you've been alone way too long. If you don't do something about it soon, you're liable to dry up and blow away."

Dixie rolled her eyes. "Lovely thought. I'll leave you to your lunch."

She marched back into the kitchen, and there stood Wade, scraping the dishes he'd brought in from the dining room, just as he should be doing.

Dammit, didn't the man goof off or screw up or take too long on his break? Anything? Something she could yell at him about?

"What?" he asked.

"What, what?"

He shrugged. "I don't know. You looked like you wanted to say something."

"If I want to say something, I'll say it. Carrie thought you were watching me."

"Carrie? Is she the BLT?"

"Never mind," Dixie said, appalled that she'd said anything.

"She was right. I was watching you."

Great, Dixie thought. *I had to open my big mouth. Now what?* "Why?"

He grinned. "You're kidding, right?"

Over in front of the grill, Pops let out a snort of laughter.

In for a penny, she thought. "I hired you, but I still don't think you needed a job. You look like money, like you come from a background of money. And you're good-looking, to boot. A man like you can have any woman he wants. Why look at me?"

Wade watched her for so long she wanted to fidget. Finally he said, "Thanks, I think, for the compliment. If that's what it was. But in answer to your question, I repeat, you're kidding, right? A smart, pretty woman with a sense of humor, a body to die for, and an accent that sounds like warm honey? A man would have to be dead to not look."

Dixie felt as if her feet were nailed to the floor. There was fire in her cheeks, her heart was pounding and deep inside, in places she'd thought long dead, a tingling danced along nerve endings. And her brain was frozen, along with her mouth. She couldn't seem to get any words past her lips.

What did a woman say to something like that, anyway? "Uh, thank you. But I'm not available." There. That should do it.

"That's a shame, but that doesn't mean a man can't look and dream."

Dixie shook her head. Her brain started working again. "Pretty words," she told him with a smile. "As long as you do your job, I don't care what you dream about."

"Heh." Pops flipped over two burgers on his grill. "Guess you lost that round, son."

"Pops," Dixie protested.

"I'd call it a draw," Wade decided.

"Hey, Wade." Tate bounded into the kitchen with Ben on his heels.

"Hey, Tater. Hey, Ben."

"Hey," Ben said.

"It's Tuesday. You gonna come watch me play ball tonight?" Tate swung an invisible bat at an imaginary pitch.

Wade swallowed around the sudden lump in his throat. Tate wanted him to come to his game. He felt humbled to be asked. The kid could not know how much it meant to him. "You play tonight?"

"You bet. Six o'clock. You comin'?"

"I wouldn't miss it."

Pops set a platter in the order window and rang the bell so Dixie would know the food was ready. "Why don't we swing by that fancy new apartment of yours and pick you up?" he suggested.

Wade chuckled. He didn't know why Pops wanted

to nudge him toward Dixie, but it certainly seemed that he did. He didn't think Dixie would appreciate it, however. Plus, Wade had to get in at least a couple of miles walking to keep up the bare minimum of exercise he needed to ward off the effects of his medications.

"Thanks," he told Pops. "But I'll meet you there."

"Suit yourself," Pops said. "As long as you're sure."

"I'm sure."

The crowd at the ball field looked like the same one from Ben's game the week before. Which made sense, since Tate's team of eight-year-olds was undoubtedly made up of the younger brothers of the ten-year-olds on Ben's team.

Wade liked it that so many people—nearly thirty, by his count—came to a Little League game on a weeknight. For a town as small as Tribute, thirty was a sizable crowd. It said something about the community, something good and solid, he thought, that not only the parents of the players came, but siblings and friends, aunts and uncles.

The sun dipped low in the west, the breeze was light and there wasn't a cloud in the sky. The temperature rested pleasantly somewhere around skin temperature. Perfect weather for outdoor sports.

"Up here."

Wade would recognize that raspy voice anywhere. "Hey, Pops."

"Saved a seat for you."

If a man wasn't careful, Wade thought, he could get used to being treated as part of the family. He climbed up into the bleachers and took a seat next to Pops. Dixie sat on Pops's other side.

Young boys ran all over the field like ants with no purpose. The game hadn't started yet. Tate's team wore green T-shirts; the other, orange.

On his walk across town to the ballpark Wade had searched inside himself for answers. Was he genuinely fond of the McCormick family, or was what he felt for them some remnant of feeling that came to him via Jimmy McCormick's donated heart?

He knew if he posed such an idea aloud, people, even doctors, would be sending him in for a psych evaluation. But there truly was such a thing as cellular memory. He had experienced it firsthand when he woke from his surgery with a healthy new heart beating in his chest and worry for his "boys" filling his mind.

But how far did cellular memory go? Was he falling head over heels for Ben and Tate, or was he just feeling Jimmy's love for them? What about his affection for Pops? Was it his, or Jimmy's?

Then he acknowledged Dixie, sitting beside Pops. He liked her. She was pretty and smart and funny. He respected her. Admired her. Those feelings were surely his own. And the attraction. There was no reason he wouldn't be attracted to her if he had someone else's heart other than her ex-husband's. So it was real. It was his. Wasn't it?

"If you don't wave back," Pops said, motioning toward the field, "his arm's gonna fall off."

"Oh, sorry." Immediately he waved to Tate down on the field. The youngster was, indeed, about to wave his arm off. "Hey, Tate!"

"Wade!" Tate bounced over toward the stands. "You came!"

"Said I would. Are you any good?"

"Sure! Mom taught me."

"Ah, well, that would do it, all right."

"Darn right it would," Dixie claimed.

Since Ben was on the top row of the bleachers with friends, this time it was Wade who made the drink run to the concession stand. By the time he returned with beer for the three of them, the game was just starting.

He was surprised and confused to see an adult on the pitcher's mound, throwing the first pitch.

"Who's that?" he asked Pops. "What's he doing?"

"Benny Lopez," Pops said. "He's our team coach. He does the pitching."

"Why?"

"Under Little League rules, seven- and eight-year-olds don't pitch. They don't have the strength and co-ordination to get the ball from the pitcher's mound to home plate."

"Yeah, I can see that. But why doesn't the pitcher just move closer to the batter?"

"'Cuz then he's too likely to get hit by the ball coming back at him if the batter connects."

"So the coach does the pitching."

"Right. Some towns have a pitching machine for these younger players. Say they're the best transition between T-ball and live pitch. But they're costly, and we'd need two of them, and a place to store them off-season."

"Costly, huh?" Wade sipped his beer. The town didn't have the money?

Ideas stirred in his mind.

Down on the field, Tate's team won the coin toss and lined up on the bench, presumably in batting order, while the opposing coach threw a couple of practice pitches.

Wade had money. More than he could spend in a lifetime even if he was trying to empty his coffers. Why should seven- and eight-year-olds do without?

Of course, nobody was saying that a machine was better than a coach. That angle merited investigation. There had to be some benefit for the batter to see an intense pair of eyes staring back at him from the pitcher's mound. Had to get used to that.

On the other hand, a nice, consistent pitch might help develop a batter's skill.

Or not. What the hell did he know about it? He would wait and learn. And ask.

The first kid up to bat swung hard and connected, but the ball fouled out.

"Do the teams want a pitching machine?"

"I'd have to say yeah. Ever since they played in

that tournament at Waco. They had a machine. Our kids have been pea green ever since. Come on, Davy, take a bite out of it!"

Young Davy took his bite and popped a fly straight down the third base line. The orange shirt on third base, however, shied away from getting underneath it. Instead, he let it bounce, allowing Davy to make it to first.

Davy probably could have made it to second—the third baseman had skinny arms and didn't look like he could throw a ball all the way to second—but Davy stuck on first despite the advice being yelled at him from the stands.

The next batter hit a single, then Tate stepped up to the plate.

"Here we go, Tate!" Dixie clapped her hands, then cupped them around her mouth to yell again. "Hit a good one!"

"Come on, Tater!" Pops hollered.

"Show 'em how!" Wade added.

At home plate, Tate hefted the bat, then turned and waved at the stands, then, with a Cheshire cat grin, took a little bow.

"What a ham." Pops chuckled. "You gotta love a kid who's that big a ham."

Yeah, Wade thought. You gotta love him.

Tate's team won their game by one point.

When the game ended, Pops offered Wade a ride

to the Dairy Queen, as was the custom. But this time Wade begged off. He didn't want to push himself into their family to the point that he made a nuisance of himself.

"I'll walk," he insisted to Pops.

Dixie, Wade noticed, did not take part in the invitation. She was turned around calling to Ben up in the top row.

"You sure?" Pops asked him.

"Yeah. I like to walk, Pops. Especially when the weather's this nice."

He made sure he found Tate before leaving the ballpark. The boy had specifically invited him to the game. Wade didn't want the boy to think he'd walked out on him.

"Wade, Wade, did you see me slide home?" Tate was sweaty, mussed and covered with red dust from head to toe. And grinning for all he was worth.

"Sure did, kiddo. You were awesome."

"Gee, thanks." Tate stretched sideways to peer behind Wade. "Where's Mom and Pops?"

"They're coming." Wade pointed a thumb over his shoulder to show Tate that Dixie and Pops were just then exiting the bleachers, with Ben right behind them.

"Cool. You're coming with us to the DQ, aren't you?"

"I'll see you there," Wade said.

"Okay. Cool. Wade?"

"Yeah?"

"Um, I'm glad you came."

Here came that lump in Wade's throat again. He did his best to swallow around it. "Yeah," he managed. "Me, too. If you get to the DQ before me, don't eat all the ice cream."

Tate snorted and giggled. "How much do they have?"

"I don't know, but you leave me some, you hear?"

"Hey, Ben!" He hopped and skipped over to meet his brother. "Wade says I have to leave some DQ ice cream for him. Did you see me get that last run? Did ya? It was the winning run!"

"Yeah, well." Ben gave him a brotherly punch in the shoulder. "I guess you did okay, for a little spud."

The idea that formed in Wade's head during the game burrowed in deeper as he enjoyed an ice cream cone at the DQ. There he met Tater's coach, Benny Lopez, who was also a volunteer firefighter. Wade found that interesting. He'd walked past the firehouse a few times during his walks and had wondered how such a small town could afford such a large facility.

"Oil," Lopez said. "The last boom we had in the area put a lot of money in the town coffers. Got us a new firehouse, a new fire engine and a new fire chief. He gets a salary. The rest of us are volunteers."

"I hope you don't get called out often," Wade said.

"More often than we'd like."

They announced Wade's order number over the

PA system. He shook hands with Lopez, then went to get his ice cream, that idea growing larger in his head. He was so preoccupied with it that he didn't realize someone was directly behind him until he turned around and ran smack into Dixie.

"Umph."

"Damn, Dixie, I'm sorry. You okay?"

"Well I was."

What did that mean? She just stared at him. "What?"

She laughed. "I'm sorry. I was kidding. I'm fine. I was just going to get a drink to go. We're headed home."

"I'll see you tomorrow, then."

"Before you go…" She put a hand on his arm and led him a few feet away from the crowd around the pickup window. "I'd like to ask you a question."

The spot on his arm where her hand touched him radiated warmth. "Sure." He imagined he could feel her fingers against his skin, even through the sleeve of his shirt. "Ask away."

Dixie frowned, trying to think of the best way to ask her question without offending or embarrassing him.

To be honest, there were several things on her mind. He'd barely looked at her during the game. He'd sat on the other side of Pops and kept his attention on the field. That should have made her happy.

It hadn't.

Of course, she hadn't so much as said boo to him, either. Maybe she'd put him off earlier at the diner when she'd told him to get back to work. Maybe he'd taken her seriously. Thought she hadn't enjoyed their flirting.

Perhaps, she thought, she had enjoyed it a little too much. But she couldn't remember the last time she'd flirted with a man she hadn't grown up with. Probably because it had never happened.

If only she knew him a little better. Knew who he was, what kind of man he was.

"What's on your mind, Dixie?" he asked quietly.

She heaved a sigh. In for a penny, in for a pound. "Please don't take this the wrong way, but most single men your age wouldn't be the least bit interested in hanging out at Little League games or ice cream parties."

"And you're wondering why I'm here?"

She shrugged. "Yeah. I'm wondering."

He looked at her thoughtfully for a moment. "I've never spent much time—no time, really—in a small town like this. The sense of community…it's very strong, and it's everywhere. The sense of freedom, the slower pace of life than in the city. The quiet, even in a yelling crowd. I'm finding it fascinating. I enjoy the ball games, and I enjoy the large and small dramas that go on in the stands." He shrugged and took a lick of his ice cream to catch a big drip before it fell. "I don't know if I'm saying what I mean, but does it answer your question? I like being around families and communities. And I'm not going to the games to hit on you, just in case you're wondering."

She blinked. "Oh, I thought…never mind."

"What *did* you think?"

"I don't know. I just wondered, that's all. I like it that you enjoy hanging out with us."

"You do?" His pulse sped up.

"How do you feel about fishing?"

"I haven't done any since I was a kid."

"We're going Sunday after church. The boys and Pops and me. We'd like it if you went with us. We've got whatever gear you might need, and I'm packing a picnic lunch for us."

"How can I turn that down?"

She had lost her mind. That was the only conclusion Dixie could draw after asking her dishwasher, for crying out loud, to a family picnic.

Oh, my God, she thought. Did she really think that way? That a dishwasher somehow wasn't, what, worthy of her?

Dixie stared at her reflection in the bathroom mirror and slapped cleansing cream onto her face.

"Snob. That's what you are."

No. That wasn't true. She was grasping at straws—as if his being her dishwasher, or any other employee, put him below her, beneath her—

Beneath her. Now, didn't that phrase conjure up a pretty picture in her head? Wade Harrison, beneath her. In bed.

"Oh, good grief." She smeared the cleansing

cream around all over her face with jerky motions. What had she been thinking to invite him?

You were thinking Carrie was right, you've got the hots for him.

That, of course, was ridiculous. It had been so long since she'd had the hots for a man, she couldn't even remember it. So what was it about this man that made her invite him into the bosom of her family, so to speak?

Ah, there it was. A tightness in her chest eased. She wet her washcloth and started cleaning off her face. She hadn't done it for herself, she'd done it for the boys. Because they liked Wade so much. Because they needed a good male influence now and then.

Not that Pops wasn't a great influence on them. A wonderful, loving influence. But he was their great-grandfather. He kept up with them, but every year it was getting harder on him. And he liked Wade as much as the boys did.

She wasn't expecting Wade to step into their lives and take Jimmy Don's place. He wasn't anything like her ex.

Jimmy Don had been a lovable Teddy bear. If you looked up *good ol' boy* in the dictionary, his picture would be there. He'd loved his sons, he'd loved her. He'd been her best friend since first grade.

He had also been the most irresponsible adult she'd ever known. If there were checks in the checkbook, that meant, to him, that there was money to spend. After all, there was beer to be bought, wasn't there?

If the gas tank held even a drop of gas, then the tank wasn't empty and there was no reason to stop and fill up, right?

If the electric bill was due on the fifteenth, they didn't really mean it. When the electricity inevitably got cut off, it was, "Well, hell's bells, I'd been meaning to pay the bill. They shoulda known that. We always pay eventually, don't we? What'd they have to go and cut us off for?"

But as sure as God made little green apples, his rodeo entry fees never got paid late.

Dixie had loved that irresponsible, lovable idiot her whole life, but she'd had all she could do to raise two sons, run the diner, keep house and worry about Jimmy Don breaking his neck riding broncs in some rodeo or another. He'd been as careless as he'd been good-looking. Finally, about four years ago, she'd had all she could take. Love him or not, she could no longer live with him.

She knew she'd done the right thing for all of them when Jimmy Don hadn't even acted surprised, and the boys barely questioned why Daddy was living out back with Pops now instead of staying in the house with them.

Pops, Lord love him, had never held the divorce against her. He knew his grandson as well as anyone did. "Hell, darlin'," Pops had said to her when she told him she was divorcing Jimmy Don. "I'm just surprised you put up with him this long."

She would always miss that big, lovable idiot, and she would never forget that last phone call he'd made to her the night he'd died. He'd been drinking, as usual, bragging about the great ride he was going to make the next day. His last words had been a plea for her to hug his "two best boys" for him. It was for those "two best boys" that she hurt the most over Jimmy's death.

She wasn't looking for a new husband. She wasn't even looking for a date. Just a picnic with her kids and Pops and a nice man who didn't have any family in the area.

"Oh, aren't I the nice one." She finished removing the cleansing cream, then rinsed out her washcloth. After wringing it as dry as possible, she shook it out and draped it over the shower rod. A dab of eye cream, a smear of night moisturizer, and she turned away from the mirror.

"Dammit." She turned back and glared at her reflection. "Okay, so he's hot. So I want to be around him outside the diner. So what? He's just passing through town. He'll be gone soon. No harm, no foul."

He hadn't said he was just passing through. Hadn't mentioned any plans about moving on. He just had that air about him. That air of moving on. That big-city air.

She gave herself a final glare in the mirror, then turned off the light. She'd invited him. What difference did her reasons make? What was done was done.

Chapter Four

Wade checked his hair in the mirror, then wiped his damp palms down the thighs of his jeans. It came as a shock to realize he was nervous. More nervous than the day he'd first walked into Dixie's Diner, hoping to gather information about the boys.

Years of board meetings, shareholders meetings, press and media interviews, the occasional congressional testimony—none of those held a candle to going on a picnic with James Donald McCormick's family.

His feelings for them were growing deep. He felt as if he'd known Pops all his life. Known, truly liked and bore a deep fondness for.

He was attracted to Dixie, and had examined his feelings for her for days. In addition to attraction, there was respect, admiration, and a strong liking, different from what he felt for Pops. This was a man-woman liking.

The boys…he didn't have to examine his feelings for them. He flat-out loved them. No two ways about it. He didn't think it mattered whether the feeling came from himself or from the new heart beating in his chest. The heart was his now. Whatever he felt, it came from him—Wade Harrison.

The growl of an engine barreled down his quiet street and slowed to an idle in front of his small apartment.

Dixie had told him not to bring anything but himself, so he stuffed his keys into his front pocket and stepped outside.

They made a picture, these McCormicks, in their big, gas-guzzling SUV. Pops sat behind the wheel, Dixie rode shotgun. The boys leaped out of the rear side door, demanding that Wade sit between them. He settled in the backseat with Ben on his right, Tate on his left.

"Good morning," Dixie greeted.

"'Morning. Where are we going?" he asked.

"To our pond," Tate announced.

"Your pond? You have a pond?"

Dixie glanced back at them and smiled.

"It was our dad's pond," Ben explained.

"Our dad's quarter section," Tate said. "Now it's ours."

"Did he used to take you guys fishing at the pond? Your dad, I mean."

"Yeah, when we were little," Ben said.

"When you were just kids, huh?" Wade winked at him. "Are there any fish in this pond?"

"You bet. There's perch, bluegill—"

"And catfish," Tate added. "And snakes and turtles, and ducks, but they usually fly away. So do the geese."

"Sounds like a busy place."

"Nah," Ben said. "It's quiet."

Ben hadn't been kidding. It *was* quiet at the pond. If you didn't count the wind and the birds and the frogs and the mooing of one cow after another as the eight or ten head of bovine across the fence greeted them.

Both boys jumped out and opened the gate in the barbwire fence. Pops drove through on the dirt drive, and there the grass took over, some of it nearly as tall as the boys. After the boys closed the gate and hopped back in, Pops took off across the grass at an angle, heading toward a scattering of trees near the far corner.

"You'll like the pond," Ben told him.

"Yeah," Tate agreed. "It's cool. It's got a fishing pier and everything."

Wade saw as they pulled up and parked beneath a huge cottonwood that someone had built a wooden pier extending about six feet out over the water and running approximately ten to twelve feet along the bank. The red, muddy water lapped more than a foot below.

"Here we are," Dixie said.

All four doors popped open at once. The boys took off for the pond.

"Hey, you two," Dixie called. "Get back here and help unload."

The boys took a few more running leaps, which put them at water's edge next to the pier and sent three frogs plopping into the pond. The boys danced around for a few seconds, staring down at the water, then, grinning wide, turned and raced back to do what they'd been told.

The family had unloading and setting things up down to a fine art. Dixie was as organized at this as she was at the diner. Within a matter of minutes, with everyone following the orders she issued in rapid-fire manner, everything was done.

Wade blinked. Beneath the cottonwood nearest the pond sat a row of three lawn chairs next to a large quilt spread out on the ground. On the quilt sat an ice chest filled with juice and soft drinks, a couple of paper sacks containing lunch makings, and a stack of towels and rags. Fishing gear rested on the wooden dock a few feet away.

Several yards away, out in the open, lay the trunks of two fallen trees. Near them lay a blackened ring of rocks obviously used to contain many a fire.

As if on signal, Ben and Tate simultaneously pounced on the ice chest and each pulled out a drink.

"This is a serve-yourself picnic," Dixie told Wade. "I'll make sandwiches later. You want anything before then, you're on your own."

"Boy," he muttered. "The service sure went downhill."

"I heard that," she said. "Service didn't go downhill, it took the day off."

"Yeah?" Pops wanted to know. "How do I get the day off?"

"Easy," she answered. "Don't catch any fish." To Wade she said, "He has to fry whatever they catch."

"That's because she doesn't do it right," Pops complained. "She's always gotta add flour to the cornmeal, and everybody knows it's better if you roll the fish in plain cornmeal."

"At least I got you to quit using salt on it," Dixie fired back.

"I can see you two are serious about your fish frying," Wade said.

"If there's anything in this world worth getting serious about," Pops told him, "it's a fish fry." The old man gave him a fake glare and raised his fists as if to fight.

"Hey." Wade put his hands up in surrender. "You won't get an argument out of me."

Pops nodded sharply. "Good enough, then."

"Come on, Pops," Tate called from the dock. "Before we catch all the fish!"

"More potato salad?"

Wade pooched out his cheeks like an overstuffed squirrel. "No, thanks. I don't think there's room. Everything was delicious."

"Thanks." Her smile teased at him.

Wade smiled back. "Ahh. You made it? Not Pops?"

"I honestly can cook," she claimed. "At home he eats my cooking every day without complaint. He just doesn't like the way I fry fish. But if I fixed it my way, I guarantee he'd eat it. He'd complain about it, but he'd eat it."

They sat for a while, the two of them, in companionable silence, and watched Pops and the boys on the pier. Out in the sunlight it was downright hot, but the air where they sat in the shade of the cottonwood was soft and warm and stirred slightly by the breeze.

"This is a pretty place," Wade said. And she was a pretty woman. The wind teased her hair. Every few minutes she brushed errant strands out of her face. Dappled light, filtered through the cottonwood leaves, drew shifting patterns across her face, her arms, the quilt. "I can see why you like to come here." Personally, he could have sat there with her forever.

"Yes." Dixie took in a deep breath, let it out. "One of the best things Jimmy Don ever did was hang on to this land. I didn't think he had it in him. He wasn't one to hold on to things," she explained. "Came as a shock when he died and we found out he still owned this place."

"You thought he'd sold it?"

"You'd have to have known my ex to understand what a big deal his keeping this land really was. Jimmy Don rarely had two cents to rub together. Money slid through his hands like water."

"You didn't know that about him when you married him?" Wade closed his eyes and shook his head. "Sorry. Not my business."

Dixie laughed. "You're right, it's not. But, yes, I knew that about him when I married him. He'd been my boyfriend since first grade."

"First grade, wow."

"Yeah." She arched her neck and looked up at the sky. "Wow. We went steady for twelve years, but were married for only nine. You ever been married?"

"Me? No."

"It's not that I don't believe you, but that seems incredible."

Wade grinned. "Is that a compliment?"

"I don't know. I guess so."

"Then thank you. But why does it seem incredible?"

"Fishing for more?"

"Fishing?" With a groan, Wade rolled his eyes toward the pier.

"Okay, sorry. No pun intended. But let's face it. You're a good-looking guy."

"Aw, shucks, ma'am," he said in his best imitation of a Texas drawl.

"Too good-looking for your own good, maybe," she added.

"And that means I should have been married by now?"

"Why not? You look like you could have any woman you want. What the devil are you doing in Podunk, Texas, hanging around somebody like me?"

"Hey, don't sell yourself short, boss. What do you mean, somebody like you?"

She shrugged. "You know. Single mother, average looks, workaholic."

Wade shook his head slowly. "You obviously don't see yourself the way I see you."

"Oh? And how is that?"

"Now who's fishing for compliments?" he teased.

"Touché."

"But to answer your question—"

"No, please." She rolled her eyes and waved her hands. "Forget I asked."

"If you get to embarrass me, I get to embarrass you," he said with a smile.

"I didn't notice you blushing."

"I was blushing on the inside."

"Do tell."

"You're trying to sidetrack me."

"Is it working?"

Wade looked her right in the eye. "When I look at you I see a very attractive woman who works her butt off—and I hope you don't mind my saying, a very fine butt it is—to run her thriving business and provide for her sons. She's strong and determined and kind and—"

Dixie blushed and looked away. "Okay, okay, but you still don't get a raise."

So, Wade thought, she wasn't comfortable accepting compliments. Did that mean she hadn't received her fair share of them in the past? He didn't want to think that his new heart came from an idiot, but…

No, he wouldn't think that. They'd gone together practically their entire lives. It would have been a miracle if they hadn't taken each other for granted.

"Got another one!"

Wade and Dixie looked to the pier and Ben, who had yelled.

"Easy, easy," Pops cautioned.

"Don't wanna lose that sucker," Tate added.

Wade and Dixie looked at each other and smiled at something that sounded like Pops coming from the eight-year-old's mouth.

"Easy," Pops said again. "That's it, that's it. Whooee! He's a beaut, Benny boy."

"Mom, Mom! Look!" Ben held out his line with the catfish still flopping around on the hook.

"Good job," Dixie called. "Be careful getting the hook out."

"Gol', Mom, I'm not a baby," he said with disgust.

"Of course you're not. I say the same thing to Pops, you know. How many is that?"

"Two for me and one for Tate," Ben called.

"They're not gonna leave any for me," Pops complained. "Watch out, there," he added to Ben. He reeled in his line and laid his pole down. "Let's use my pliers to get that hook out. That ol' catfish'll cut you to pieces if he can."

"Didn't I just tell him to be careful?" Dixie mumbled. "When it comes from me, he gets all bent out of shape. From Pops, it's great."

"That's because you're a girl," Wade offered. "Don't take it personally, Mom. Guys don't take advice from girls when other guys are around."

For Dixie it was a slow, lazy, absolutely wonderful day, made more so because of Wade's presence. Who would have thought that adding an extra man to the outing could make such a difference?

Look at him, she thought, sitting there beside the fire toasting marshmallows with her sons.

The sun was just going down, the air was cooling.

They had all stuffed themselves on catfish. She'd brought potatoes, which they'd wrapped in foil and cooked over the hot coals.

The watermelon had been a big hit, even though it was too early in the season to get a really good one.

But the pleasure for Dixie was in watching her sons enjoy Wade's company. She had worried that Pops might feel shut out, or somehow replaced. But he, too, seemed to be enjoying Wade's presence.

To be honest—and Dixie tried to be honest— Wade's interaction with the men in her life was only part of the reason she was enjoying herself so much. The fact that he was a great-looking guy who flirted with her at every turn had a lot to do with it.

Okay, she was vain and self-centered and obviously more starved for male companionship than she'd realized.

But, oh, he was fine to look at. Sexy, funny and so caring with Ben and Tate.

How could she stop herself from caring about him? Why should she even try?

At that precise moment he looked across the fire, and their gazes met. Dixie felt heat seep through her body, even as the air left her lungs. She wanted to lick her lips, but at the last second stopped herself. Her mouth was just as dry as her lips, anyway.

Pulling her gaze away took much more effort than it should have. She cleared her throat. "It'll be dark soon. We need to start packing up."

"Aw, Mom."

"Aw, Mom."

"Yeah," Wade said. "Aw, Mom."

"Very funny, you three." But she laughed. "Tate, you help Pops load up the fishing gear. Ben, take the bucket and get water to put out the fire."

"What about me," Wade asked as everyone scattered. "What can I do?"

"You don't need to do anything. You're our guest."

"And I'm glad to be your guest." He walked around the fire, came steadily toward her until they were a mere two feet apart. He reached out and placed his hands on her shoulders.

Dixie couldn't control the shiver that raced through her at his touch. His hands were warm and deliciously heavy. Her pulse sped.

"I can't remember when I've had so much fun," he said quietly.

"Wade." She had no idea what she might have said next. He was so close he seemed to swallow up all the air, because she couldn't quite draw in enough. She was grateful when he interrupted her.

"Or better fish." He dropped his hands to his sides and took a step back. "Now I'll help load up. I'll get the lawn chairs." He turned away and folded up the lawn chairs.

When he walk away toward the SUV, carrying the three lawn chairs, Dixie shook her head. What the hell was the matter with her? She'd practically swooned at his feet like some helpless Southern belle.

"Idiot," she muttered.

"Did you say something, Mom?"

Dixie jumped as if she'd been shot. There stood Ben, swinging his empty bucket beside the steaming remnants of the fire. "How long have you been standing there?" Great. Now she was yelling at her kids. She was definitely losing it.

"Gol', I dunno. Whatsa matter?"

"Nothing. You just startled me, that's all. Good job on the fire. Here, take this sack up to Pops at the car, please."

"Are you sure you won't let me drive you home?" Dixie asked Wade. He had insisted on helping unload the car. All that was done now, and Pops was gone across the dark backyard to his apartment. The boys had already plopped down in front of the television. They weren't about to take their baths without being told. Their desertion left her alone in the kitchen with Wade. She wanted a little more time with him. Maybe if she drove him home he would touch her again. Or she would get brave enough to touch him. But in the end, he turned down her offer.

"After all that fish," he said, "I feel a need for a walk."

"I know what you mean." Dixie smiled despite her disappointment. "I'm glad you came with us today."

"So am I. Like I said earlier, I had a great time. You've got a couple of really terrific kids."

"Thank you. I think they're pretty great, too."

She led the way from the kitchen into the living room. Ben lay sprawled on his belly on the carpet beside the coffee table, his neck bent up sharply to see the television. Tate had the couch, but instead of sitting on it, he had his stocking feet on the wall behind the couch, his butt backward in the seat, and his head hanging off the seat cushion so he had to watch the TV upside down.

Dixie let out a mother's sigh, a combination of love and dismay. "Say good-night to Wade, boys."

There was silence for a moment, except for the squealing of tires in the car chase on TV.

"Boys?"

A commercial came on the air. Both boys flipped over to look at Wade.

"Do you have to go?" Ben asked.

"Can't he stay?" Tater begged.

"Hey, thanks, guys," Wade said before Dixie could speak. "But I've gotta get home and get my beauty rest."

The boys snickered and made gagging noises.

Dixie opened the front door and stepped out onto the porch. Wade said good-night to the boys and followed. He stood next to her, with the only light on the dark porch coming from the open front door behind him and the streetlight down the block. Two houses away, a dog barked. Such a normal sound. But Dixie didn't feel normal. She felt…expectant. She wanted—

"What?" Wade asked.

"What, what?"

"You looked like you wanted to say something."

Dixie chuckled. "Didn't we have this conversation earlier today?"

"It does sound familiar, albeit reversed. So, what's on your mind?"

She was tired of this seesawing of her emotions, of not knowing what to do about it. Of denying herself. She decided to go for it.

"I've been thinking," she began.

"About what?"

"About kissing."

He made a choking sound.

"No comment?"

He cleared his throat. "Just wondering if you're a mind reader."

"Nice save," she told him, her heart starting to race.

"What is it about kissing that you were thinking about?" he asked.

"Well." She took a swaying step toward him, trying to act as if she knew what she was doing, all the while praying she wasn't making a fool of herself. "It occurred to me that if I were to kiss you, it could be construed—since I'm your boss, I mean— as sexual harassment."

He took a step toward her, leaving a scant inch of night air between them. "I never thought of that."

"Oh, I did."

He lowered his face toward hers. "You have to know I'd never complain if you kissed me."

"That is good to know." She tilted her face up. Her breath mingled with his. "But, we wouldn't have to worry about it at all, if…" She used her tongue to moisten her lips.

He made a quiet moaning sound. "If?" His lips were all but touching hers.

Hers were practically vibrating. "If…you… kissed…me."

"Ah." He moved a fraction of an inch closer. "I see the difference. You…don't mind?"

"Mind?" She swallowed hard. "Mind what?"

"This." His lips brushed over hers so lightly, she wasn't sure she felt him.

Then again and again, teasing her, tasting her, each time more firmly, more fully. Yet still teasing.

Dixie wanted more, a deeper taste. She took his face in both hands and held him closer. And took what she wanted from him.

And he gave it. His heat, and his arms, surrounded her. His taste, the sharp, sweet flavor of man, delighted her. The way he pulled her body to his and held her close turned her knees to jelly.

Deeper and deeper he took them, and she reveled in it. There were no neighbors who could see if they looked out their windows. There were no children just inside the door. There was no employee to face in the morning. There was only now, the two of them. No world, just his mouth, his hands, his thighs. The hardness of his…

One more minute and she would be begging him to take her right there on her front porch. To forestall that, she reluctantly ended the kiss and inched back from him.

He let out a long breath. "That was…"

"Yeah. It was."

"I should let you go in," he said.

"I should go in," she said.

"Good night."

"Okay." Her brain was still scrambled. The man's kiss packed a punch. "Just one more."

"Oh, good." And he took her in his arms again and kissed her. It was long and slow and deep, and she wanted it to never end.

But this time it was Wade who ended it and stepped back. He squeezed her shoulders gently. "If I don't leave right now, we could end up shocking your sons."

"Good night," she told him, not sure if her heart would ever slow to normal again.

"Good night."

Dixie stood on the porch and watched as Wade walked down the street and disappeared into the darkness.

Oh, man, she thought. She pressed her hands to her heated cheeks and wondered how she was supposed to face him in the morning. Without jumping his bones.

Wade smiled all the way home. He purposely blocked the questions and concerns trying to seep into the forefront of his mind. It was easy for a while, because he kept reliving the day, the kiss. Especially the kiss. The first one, the second one.

Dixie had surprised him. After treating him more or less like a member of the family for most of the day, she could have given him a good-night handshake and he wouldn't have been surprised or offended.

But she must have been feeling the same pull and heat that had been stalking him. For which he would be eternally grateful.

Now, however, what was she going to think...how was he going to tell her why he'd come to Tribute? Did this change why he was here?

Hell, he'd been telling himself since before he left New York that he was coming to Texas to check on the boys.

Okay. He'd checked on them. They had a good life, a great mother, a fine town and a terrific great-grandfather for a male role model. They didn't need Wade. He had no excuse for staying. Yet he couldn't imagine leaving.

Not yet. He couldn't leave just yet. Something

felt unfinished. The boys never talked about their dad, but that didn't mean anything. They'd been without him for two years now. Why should they talk about him?

Dixie had spoken briefly about him today, but, while she'd obviously cared for her ex, she hadn't exactly raved about what a great guy he'd been.

So the man had been human. So he hadn't been the perfect husband. He'd loved his sons, and surely their mother, too. Sometime during his life he'd done the courageous thing and checked the organ donor box on his driver's license. It was that act, that one deed, that made the man a hero in Wade's book. It was for that, and not his inability to pay his bills, that he should be remembered.

Many people were terrified to check that box. They thought it meant that if they were ever seriously injured, some overeager doctor would see that check mark and start harvesting organs, guaranteeing the injured person's premature demise. A primal nightmare, waking up while your heart was being cut out.

To be honest, before his own heart trouble, Wade had barely been able to force himself to check that box. He wasn't above a primal nightmare or two of his own.

But when he needed a heart, there was James Donald McCormick, hero extraordinaire. He may have had too much to drink, he may have stepped carelessly in front of a cab—according to Wade's investigation, that's what had happened. But sometime before that, Jimmy Don, as his family called him, had stepped up to the plate and checked that little box that had saved Wade's life.

Wade had been lucky, and he knew it. He could think of no way to express how he felt about his donor, no way to make the man's sons see their father as the hero he was, above and beyond a father's normal heroic status, to tell them how many lives he'd saved, how many other lives he had improved by his generous gifts.

How was he supposed to do that after the way he'd kissed Dixie tonight?

Maybe, he thought as he let himself into his apartment, some solution would come to him during the night. He had time yet. There was no clock ticking on when he told them who he was, or if he even told them at all, as long as they came to see their father the way Wade wanted them to.

But he was wrong about there being no deadline. After listening to his voice mail that night, he could hear, along with his sister's voice, the ticking of a giant clock.

"Wade," she'd said, "dammit, of all the times for you to turn off your cell phone. Well, it can't be helped. You need to know that the tabloids have discovered you're missing. It's only a matter of time before they track you down, so hurry up and finish your business and get home."

Chapter Five

"Mom?"

"What is it, hon?" Dixie stood in her kitchen and smoothed a hand over Tate's unruly hair.

"How come you're only wearing one shoe?"

Dixie looked down and sighed. *Well, damn.* "Because I'm old and forgetful."

"Ha!" Pops cackled. "If you're old, what's that make me? Time to get to work, you guys. As soon as your mother finishes getting dressed."

Dixie rolled her eyes and went in search of her other shoe. It had been like that since she woke up.

Longer. Her mind had been in a fog since she'd watched Wade walk away last night. She'd almost let the boys go to bed without a bath. This morning she'd tried to put two earrings into the same hole in her ear. She'd brushed her teeth without toothpaste. And now she'd nearly left the house wearing only one shoe.

All this because of one kiss. Okay, two, but who was counting? Two kisses from a man who took her breath away.

Had it really been so long since she'd been with a man that a couple of kisses could knock her for such a loop?

The answer was yes. The last man she'd been with had been Jimmy Don, about a year after their divorce, when she'd had one too many beers and he'd been exceptionally charming.

Now here she was, three years later, going gaga over a couple of kisses.

When she and Pops and the kids finally arrived at the diner, she breathed a sigh of relief that Wade wasn't standing outside waiting for them. She still had time to decide how to act around him.

About three minutes, as it turned out. Not nearly enough time to prepare herself for seeing Wade again. She sent the boys off to the banquet room, then turned toward the kitchen to help Pops with their breakfast. And suddenly there was Wade, already standing at the counter checking the supplies she would need during the day.

He was so damned good-looking, she thought. All she could do was stand there and drink him in with her eyes.

"Hi," he said, his attention barely straying from checking the level in each ketchup bottle.

"Good morning." Lord, did she have to sound so breathy? She cleared her throat. "No trouble getting home last night?"

He glanced at her, smiled quickly. "Not a bit."

Yes, and, hello, my name's Dixie. What's yours? He was acting as if he barely knew her. She suddenly felt unsure of herself, and it was not a comfortable feeling. "Is anything wrong?"

"Not a thing. Everything seems in order here. I'm going to go put these bottles out on the tables."

"Sure. Okay." She didn't know what else to say. "Good." And wasn't that brilliant?

Once again she reminded herself that Wade could have any woman he wanted. She'd wondered why he would be interested in her. Now, it seemed, he wasn't.

She sniffed. Okay. She didn't have to let it bother her. She went to the kitchen and sipped coffee while she helped Pops fix Ben's and Tate's breakfasts.

From the time Dixie turned over the open sign, customers started pouring in. It seemed that everyone in town was hungry this morning. The earlybirds had already cleared out and their replacements were sipping a final cup of coffee when she saw Wade leave the kitchen and make his way to the banquet room.

She'd have to thank him for that. She hadn't had

time to clean up after Ben and Tate, and Wade was doing it for her.

She finished taking an order for a Denver omelette, then turned it in to Pops and picked up an empty tub to bus the front corner booth.

"Dixie?"

She turned sharply at Wade's soft call. He held the kitchen door open and stepped out.

She moved toward him so they wouldn't have to yell at each other. "Yes?"

"One of the boys left this in the booth back there."

Dixie recognized the math book Wade held as Ben's. His homework pages were sticking out. She groaned in frustration. "That boy. I think his math class starts around nine-thirty. Well, I can't leave to take it to him, so he'll just have to do without and take his lumps."

"I could take it to him," Wade offered.

"As busy as we are, you're needed here," she countered.

"It's what, a ten-minute walk to the grade school? You're not going to run out of dishes before I get back."

Dixie studied his face for a moment and realized he was serious. "Are you sure you wouldn't mind?"

He smiled. "Of course I wouldn't mind. I volunteered, didn't I?"

A tightness in Dixie's chest eased at his smile. "Okay. Thanks. Ben will owe you a big favor for this."

Wade chuckled. "I'll tell him you said so."

* * *

Despite everything that weighed on Wade's mind, he couldn't help but smile. He'd never walked to school before, and here he was, an adult with a math book under his arm doing that very thing. It was scarcely nine o'clock, yet the temperature was already rising and the humidity was up. But the sky was gloriously blue, and the traffic—well, every now and then a car went by.

He'd been right that it would take him ten minutes to reach the elementary school. The redbrick building was long and low, with a large gymnasium on one end and a fenced playground on the other. In the center of the building sat the main entrance, complete with a covered walkway.

Wade chose to enter through the door near the gym because it was closer, and it was propped open. When he stepped inside, he realized why. The floor was wet.

"Watch your step," a man called out.

Wade glanced down the connecting hallway that ran the length of the school and saw a janitor pushing an industrial-size mop back and forth across the floor.

Wade stepped carefully. "Sorry to track up your clean floor, but I have a book to deliver." Something about the man tickled the back of Wade's memory. "I thought you guys did this after school."

"I do, usually, but this morning's water balloons were filled with grape Kool-Aid."

"Good one." Wade held out his hand. "Wade

Harrison. If you'd point me toward the office, I'd appreciate it."

The janitor narrowed his eyes as he held out his hand to shake. "I thought you looked familiar." Recognition shined in his eyes. "Nick Carlucci. Welcome to Tribute Elementary. And delivering a book aside, what the hell are you doing in Tribute, Texas?"

"Carlucci," Wade said softly, noting the way the man favored his left leg. "Carlucci." Firefighter. FDNY. "*That* Nick Carlucci?" The man was a legend in New York. He'd lost his father and brother when the Twin Towers collapsed, then went on to save a half-dozen or so other rescuers from a falling beam, only to have that same beam crush his spine.

What the hell was he doing mopping floors in a grade school in the middle of Texas? "I could ask you the same question."

Carlucci glanced around sharply, as if to check and make sure no one was listening. "What do you mean?"

"I mean, I know who you are. Nick Carlucci, firefighter, 9/11."

"If you'd keep that to yourself, I'd appreciate it," Carlucci said. "Around here I'm just Nick the janitor."

"Fine by me. Around here I'm just Wade the dishwasher over at Dixie's Diner."

"Ah, *that* dishwasher."

"Pardon?"

Carlucci shrugged and smiled. "Small town. Word gets around."

"What word would that be?"

"That there's a hot new studmuffin working over at the diner."

"A *what?*" Heat stung Wade's cheeks. Good God, he was blushing. Then again, it was a comment worthy of a good blush.

Carlucci raised one hand while holding on to the mop handle with the other. "Hey, man, don't shoot the messenger."

Wade ran a hand down his face, trying to rub away the embarrassment. "What are the odds, two guys from Manhattan ending up in Tribute, Texas?"

"Two guys who would just as soon everyone not know all the details of their past lives?"

Wade nodded.

"Astronomical, I'd say."

"Yeah," Wade agreed. "Hey, listen, we should both get back to work. If you'll point me to the office."

"Sure. Down the hall, right across from the main entrance."

"Thanks." Wade started past the man, then paused. "We should get together for a beer sometime." Then he thought better of it. "Or…not."

Carlucci nodded. "Yeah. Maybe not."

The fireman went back to his mopping while the CEO went looking for a ten-year-old.

A young woman behind the counter in the school's office looked up Ben's classroom and gave Wade directions. He got the book to Ben and made it back to the diner, having been gone under thirty minutes total.

"Thank you, Wade," Dixie told him.

"You're welcome." And my, he thought, how polite they'd become with each other. Polite and distant. All because he'd been unable to keep his hands and his mouth, to himself.

"Dixie," he said softly as she turned to leave.

She paused, turned her head toward him. "Yes?"

"Did I ruin things?"

She frowned "Ruin what? Ben's math book?"

"No. Things between us."

Her gaze darted away. "Don't be silly. We're still friends, aren't we? Last night was just…"

"Last night was just what?"

"It just happened, that's all. It doesn't have to change anything."

She wasn't saying what was on her mind. He could tell that from the way she refused to meet his gaze. He might consider pushing her on it, but not while she had work on her mind and Pops as an audience.

She turned and left, and he tackled the stacks of dirty dishes that had accumulated while he'd been gone.

Later that afternoon, shortly before the boys came in for their after-school snack, Wade overheard Dixie telling someone that she was sorry but there were no openings at the diner.

Wade peered through the window in the door to

the dining room and saw a middle-aged Latino man who appeared to take the news hard but silently. If he squeezed and twisted his straw cowboy hat any harder against his chest, the hat was going to end up in shreds. Wade didn't think he'd ever seen any man look that disappointed.

Pops came and looked over Wade's shoulder. "Takin' it kinda hard, looks to me."

"Yeah."

"'There but by the grace of God…'" Pops murmured.

Wade felt like a fraud. There was a man who needed a job, even a minimum-wage dishwashing job, and the only thing standing between him and a paycheck was Wade, who had more money than he could spend in three lifetimes.

Son of a bitch.

That afternoon after work, Wade took his usual walk through town. It was time, as his granddad Conrad used to say, to fish or cut bait. Or, as Grandfather Harrison would have put it, "Young man, it's time to vote or sign over your proxy."

As to the current situation, it was time he did something positive for the boys and go home. Or just go home. Yet he found himself strongly reluctant to leave Tribute. There was something he was supposed to do. He could feel it deep inside. He just didn't know what that something was. Until he figured it out, he would not leave town.

First things first, he decided as he turned the corner and started walking down Main. First meant making sure the boys were amply provided for. He pulled his cell phone from his pocket and dialed his attorney. It was after 7:00 p.m. in New York, but he didn't care. The hefty retainer he paid ought to be good for something.

"Carl, I need you to do something for me."

"All right. But first are you aware that rumors of your whereabouts are circulating rapidly?"

"Some people don't have enough to do with their time, I suppose. I want you to set up a couple of college funds for me."

"College funds?"

"That's right." He glanced around to make sure no one was close enough to him to overhear. "Fifty thousand each."

"You're sure?"

"I'm sure. My broker will know where to put it."

"All right. Names?"

He looked around again, making sure he was free from prying ears. "Ben McCormick and Tate McCormick. They can't touch it except for college, but then they can use it for tuition, books, housing, transportation, food, just about anything."

"Entertainment?"

"Sure."

"If they don't go to college?"

"They can withdraw up to half the original amount when they reach twenty-one."

"Up to twenty-five thousand, regardless of the current value of the account?"

"That's right. If something goes wrong with the investment and there's not at least twenty-five thousand still there, they can withdraw half of whatever's left. The rest gets converted to a retirement account."

"And if something happens to one or both before they reach college age, where do you want the money to go?"

"To their mother, Dixie McCormick."

"Dixie? You're kidding. Is that her legal name?"

"It is."

They firmed up a few more details. Wade would follow up with addresses and other information, then Carl would send him a draft of the details they had just discussed. If it was what Wade wanted, Carl would proceed and set up the accounts.

That took care of item number one on Wade's list of things to do. Now all he had to do was determine precisely what constituted item number two.

Dixie held her breath the next morning until the boys left the diner for school. Hoping, praying that Tate would not invite Wade to his Little League game that night. Praise God, her prayers were answered.

That didn't mean Wade wouldn't show, but that

her son hadn't invited him was the best she could hope for.

Wade had been nice yesterday, taking Ben's book to school for him, then catching up on the backlog of dirty dishes in no time at all. But that distance she'd felt yesterday morning between them was still there, and now it felt like a mile-wide gap.

She knew the man had secrets. He had an entire past that she knew nothing about. She suspected that he might be on the run, hiding from someone or something.

Then again, that could simply be her overactive imagination. She had no proof of anything being wrong.

"Boy, howdy, I guess Carrie was right."

Dixie refilled Maria Arvelos's tea and smiled. "Right about what?" The three of them, Carrie, Maria and Dixie, had known each other since first grade.

"About you being distracted. She swears it's because of your new dishwasher. What's his name?"

"Carrie is full of it. His name is Wade, and I'm not distracted."

"Oh, yeah?" Maria smirked. "Then how come you just filled my cola glass with tea?"

Dixie closed her eyes and took a deep breath. "Sorry. I'll get you a new drink."

"I'll let you, too. When you come back, be prepared to tell all."

"Ha. Don't hold your breath, girlfriend. First I'd

have to know something before I could tell it," Dixie all but growled.

"Listen," Maria said when Dixie returned with a fresh cola for her. "We need a girls' night. Can you get Pops to stay with your boys, say, Friday night?"

"Probably," Dixie said, thinking a girls' night sounded like just the thing to get her mind off a certain dishwasher.

"Of course, what we should do is go over to Terri's just about dark, or before sunup."

"Not that I wouldn't want to visit Terri, but why at dark or before sunup?"

Maria leaned toward her and lowered her voice. "Because we can watch the track."

Dixie leaned down and whispered. "Why do we want to watch the track?"

Maria sat up and made a face. "You really don't know anything, do you? That's when your dish-washer runs."

Dixie was confused. "Runs?"

"Yeah, you know, moving forward at a pace faster than walking?"

"Maria, quit dancing around the subject and spill it. What the devil are you talking about?"

At that moment a middle-aged couple entered the diner, and at the same time Wade came out of the kitchen to bus tables.

"Never mind," Maria said out of the side of her mouth. "Tell you later."

Her friend, Dixie decided, had lost her marbles.

Dixie seated the new couple, gave them menus and took their drink orders. She returned to the kitchen right after Wade. Considering Maria's comments, Dixie didn't dare look him in the eye. No way could she explain away something she didn't understand.

As it turned out, she had no need to explain anything, because Wade made no attempt to engage her in conversation. In fact, when she did finally look at him, he seemed as preoccupied with his own thoughts as she'd been with hers.

It surprised her, then, that with the way they were all but avoiding each other, and he had no specific invitation from her sons, that he turned up at Tate's game that evening.

Dixie wasn't sure why she was surprised, seeing that he'd been to every one of Ben's and Tate's games since he'd come to town. Maybe it wasn't surprise but dismay. Crushed hopes? Or maybe some part of her was worried that her boys were becoming too fond of a man none of them knew anything about.

Or maybe she was just looking for excuses to avoid facing her own feelings for him.

The wind had picked up in the two hours since she'd left work. Clouds had been piling up and rolling away, then piling up again all afternoon. They'd be lucky to make it through the game without a storm hitting.

Pops gave her a none-too-gentle nudge. "Aren't you going to invite him to sit with us?"

"Invite who?" she said, playing ignorant.

"Ha. Lie to yourself all you want, girl, but you can't fool me. You knew the minute he stepped foot in the park."

Dixie crossed her arms and glared. "Don't be ridiculous. How would I know such a thing?"

"'Cuz you've got radar, that's how. Wade radar. Looky there, you can't keep your eyes off him even while you're listening to me run off at the mouth. Might as well be talking to myself," he added, muttering.

And he was right. She couldn't keep her gaze from straying, now that she knew Wade was there. But that didn't mean she had to admit it.

"Wade radar," she muttered. "I won't even dignify that with a response."

"Seems to me you just did."

"Give it a rest, Pops."

"You know—"

"I can call myself an idiot just the same as you can," she told him with a sigh.

"Well, then. There you go. Now, invite that young man up here so he can sit with friends instead of with strangers or by himself."

"You want him up here, you invite him."

Pops didn't bat an eye. He stood and waved at Wade to come and join them.

Dixie forced a smile. She needed to snap out of whatever this mood was. Wade was her employee and, she hoped, her friend. Whatever was going on inside her little pea brain, and that included the part that managed hormones, was not worth losing a friend over.

"Hi," she said when he joined them. "I didn't know you were coming tonight."

"Wouldn't miss it."

"Here." Pops scooted away from Dixie and patted the empty space left. "Have a seat and rest your bones."

Wade looked at Dixie as if not sure of his welcome. "You don't mind?"

It was good to know, Dixie thought, that she wasn't the only one suffering from uncertainty. And it was silly that either one of them did. They were grown-ups. They worked together, and they had kissed. End of story. She offered him a smile, and this time she meant it.

"No," she told him. "I don't mind. Join us. Please."

Wade felt a tightness in his chest ease. He had come to the game out of habit, and because he didn't know what else to do with himself unless he wanted to stay home and read or drive around the countryside.

He should have stayed home and figured out what else, if anything, he was going to do regarding Ben and Tate. The college funds he'd established were plenty. His conscience would allow him to end it there and go home to New York.

But something else deep inside told him he wasn't finished in Tribute. There was something else, something vitally important left for him to do. So, for now, he would watch Little League.

He took a seat between Dixie and Pops and somehow felt right at home there. He shouldn't have been surprised. They had always made him feel welcome, from the first day. Lying to them by not telling them who he was and what he was doing there seemed a poor way to repay them. Yet he still couldn't bring himself to reveal the truth.

A sudden lull in the wind allowed the *whap* of the bat hitting the ball to sound louder than usual. There was no *crack* in Little League as there was in Major League baseball. Eight-year-old arms could not swing as hard. But the sound was no less satisfying for its lack of decibels.

The crowd cheered, and the wind slammed back, as if in response. Or maybe the wind was cheering, too.

"Way to go, Bobby!" Dixie yelled.

Now it was Tate's turn at bat. Wade felt a smile coming on as the kid started his usual antics. He held the bat above his head in both hands and faced the stands, grinning like the Cheshire cat. After he'd gotten a few hoots and hollers, he lowered the bat and took a bow.

Next to Wade, he heard Dixie groan.

"Ah, come on, Mom," he said. Forgetting they hadn't been particularly close for the past couple of days, he nudged her arm with his. "He's a kid, and he's adorable."

"And if you don't believe it," she offered, "just ask him. He'll tell you exactly how adorable he is."

Pops braced his hands on his knees and leaned forward. "Smart kid, I'd say. He knows it's a poor dog that won't wag its own tail."

"I believe," Dixie said, "he's about to do just that."

On the other side of the tall, chain link backstop, Tate stepped up to the plate. He widened his stance and bent forward. He held the bat beside his ear and poked his elbows out. He turned his head to face the pitcher.

Wade smiled in anticipation of what he knew would come next.

"Here it comes," Dixie murmured.

Even the wind hesitated, as if waiting.

The pièce de résistance: he wiggled his butt.

"That's my boy," Pops crowed.

"This," Dixie muttered, "from a kid who can't keep a Hula-Hoop up."

Tate waited, and when the pitch didn't come, he wiggled his butt again.

From somewhere in or around the stands, a young girl's voice called out, "Go, baby, go!"

Wade nearly swallowed his tongue.

Pops chortled and slapped his knee.

Dixie came to attention. "Baby?" she kept her voice to a low growl. "Some little eight-year-old hussy is calling my baby 'baby'? He's too young to be some girl's baby."

"Now, now, Mom." Wade forgot they weren't

touching each other. He smiled and patted her just above her knee. "It's just a saying."

"A saying?" She scanned the crowd through slitted eyes.

"Yeah." To be safe, he took his hand from her thigh. "You know, like, 'Atta boy,' or 'Way to go.' That sort of thing."

"Yeah, right." She shot him a look that said, Get real. "For wiggling his butt?"

"If you wiggled your butt in my direction, I'd probably get excited and yell myself."

She turned slowly to face him and arched her brow. Her eyes sparkled with a mixture of mirth and challenge. "Oh, *really?*"

He would meet that challenge. He directed his gaze to her son at home plate and smiled. "Absolutely."

The pitcher, in this case the coach, finally pitched. Tate swung and missed.

Overhead, thunder rumbled.

Wade looked up, surprised to see dark, bulging clouds hanging low in the sky. The sun wouldn't set for more than an hour, yet it looked much later.

He had experienced as many thunderstorms as the next person, but he'd managed to live his life without a tornado. Texas tended to have a lot of tornados, didn't they?

He glanced at the people in the stands, and no one seemed to be concerned with anything but whether or not Tate was going to hit the next pitch.

If no one else cared about the weather, neither would he. He looked back down at the field in time to see Tate swing and miss a second time.

"That's all right, Tate!" Dixie yelled.

"Take your time," Pops hollered. "Pick your pitch!"

The boy took his great-grandfather's advice and let the next pitch, which was so far outside it should have been a crime, go by. The next one, he fouled. The fourth, however, he connected with what might have been a line drive, had it been hit with more force, and had it gone straight. As it was, the ball rolled past the pitcher then curved out toward third, but stopped about halfway there.

Meanwhile Tate didn't wait around to see where his ball went. He ran to first. Then, because out in midfield no one could decide who should get the ball still on the ground, he ran to second.

By then the third baseman decided to get the ball, so Tate stood pat on second.

Wade felt the tension in his muscles ease and nearly laughed out loud. If his colleagues in New York, the ones who knew the old Wade, pretransplant, preheart trouble, could see him getting worked up over a Little League game, they wouldn't even recognize him.

He barely recognized himself, but he didn't care. He sat under a stormy Texas sky with a beautiful, sexy woman on one side, a wise elderly man on the other and a field full of energetic children to entertain them. What more could a man ask for?

Chapter Six

In the top half of the fourth inning the sky opened up. The only warning was a big fat drop of rain here and there. Then nothing. Then, *whoosh!* Even if anyone had an umbrella with them in the stands or out on the field, there was no time to get one up to prevent a serious soaking. This was no gentle shower, but a torrent of hard, cold bullets of water hurtling down with enough force to hurt.

The bleachers erupted in curses and shouts as spectators scrambled down the risers to race for the shelter of their vehicles. Wade followed Dixie and Pops to the end of their bench, then they started down the stairs. He saw it happen as if in slow motion and was helpless to prevent it.

Lightning shot a jagged spear from cloud to ground no more than fifty yards away. The explosive sound was deafening. The smell of sulfur stung the eyes and nostrils.

In reaction, Dixie jerked and slipped on the rain-slicked stairs. To regain her balance she waved her arms wildly, but in the process she accidentally hit Pops just hard enough to throw him off balance.

Pops's foot slipped down between the open steps. He cried out and started to fall.

Wade grabbed the back of the man's plaid shirt and pulled him back. The two of them ended up seated on the steps. Pops cried out again.

"You okay?" Wade had to raise his voice to be heard over the pounding rain.

"My ankle," he managed breathlessly.

Wade's gut tightened. "Is it broken?" God, he hoped not.

"I can still move my toes, but the ankle hurts like blazes."

"Pops?" Dixie came back for him. "What happened?"

"Slipped." Pops's mouth was ringed with a thin line of white. He was definitely in pain.

Wade tried to wipe water from his face so he could see better. "It's his ankle."

"Is it bad?" she asked. "Can you walk?"

"Of course I can," Pops said irritably. "No need to fuss."

"Don't tell me not to fuss." Dixie braced her shoulder beneath the man's right arm while Wade pushed Pops up from behind. "I'm a woman. Women fuss. It's genetic."

They got Pops upright, but his injured ankle wouldn't bear any weight. Wade took as much of the man's weight as Pops would allow. They hobbled down the last few stairs to level ground.

"What about the boys?" Pops worried.

"It's just a little rain," Dixie answered. "They won't melt." So she said, but her expression said she was worried, about them, about Pops.

"Is there a problem, folks?" Two men in EMT shirts approached holding an umbrella and carrying what looked like a red tackle box.

"Just a sprained ankle," Pops groused. "Don't know why everybody's making such a fuss."

One man squatted down and carefully pulled up Pops's pant leg. The inside of the ankle was bloody.

"Why don't you come on over to the truck and let us have a look at it?"

"Thank you," Dixie responded before Pops could deny he needed help.

The two EMTs took over and practically carried Pops to the back of their ambulance. They got him out of the rain and checked out his ankle.

"Why don't I go round up the boys," Wade offered.

"Oh, would you?" The look of gratitude on Dixie's face made him want to kiss her. But he refrained.

Wade found the boys huddled beneath the bleachers with several other kids and adults. The bleachers offered some protection, but water still streamed down between the steps. Everyone there was as soaked as he was.

"Golly, Wade, you're all wet." Tate, water running down his face, grinned.

"I am? How did that happen?"

"Where's Mom and Pops?" Ben asked.

"Pops hurt his ankle. Your mom went with him to have the EMTs look at it."

Tate scrunched up his face in worry. "Is it bad?"

"Probably not," Wade offered. "Your mom just wanted to be sure. I told her I'd come get you guys."

"You want us to go back out in that?" Ben protested.

"Yeah." Tate snorted. "Like it's so dry under here, dip weed."

A loud *crack* had everyone flinching.

"Hail," said another man under the stands with them.

Another icy ball shot down from the clouds and bounced on the hood of a nearby car. Then another and another, until the din from the hail drowned out all talk, all thought. It pelted, it roared. It hammered into the bleachers just over their heads and shot through the openings at each bench seat and step. Wade pulled Ben and Tate close and leaned over them, protecting them with his body from the hail-stones that came through the open spaces above them. And some did get through; he would have a bruise or two on his back to prove it.

The pounding went on for several minutes, then stopped as if someone had flipped a switch. Even the rain let up, nothing more than a heavy drizzle now.

Wade straightened and heaved a sigh of relief, not surprised to realize he was breathing hard. If his hands weren't already wet, he was sure they would be sweating.

"Come on, guys, lets go find your mom and Pops."

They found them inside the ambulance, out of the rain. They'd left the back doors open, so Wade and the boys leaned in to get their heads out of the rain.

One paramedic was fiddling with something inside a built-in drawer while the other squatted and worked over Pops's bared ankle. He and Pops and Dixie spoke together in low, indistinguishable tones.

"Mom?" Ben asked tentatively.

"There you two are. Thank you, Wade."

"No problem," Wade answered.

The tech poked again on Pops's ankle. Pops hissed in pain.

"Is Pops okay?" Tate asked, sounding much younger than his eight years.

"I will be," Pops said irritably, "soon as everybody quits poking and fussing."

"I don't know, Mr. McCormick," the tech said. "I

know you can still wiggle your toes, but that doesn't mean you didn't break something, or at least crack a bone or two. It's already starting to swell. We'll run you up to the hospital and get an X-ray to be sure."

"Ah, hell, I don't need no—"

Dixie cut Pops off. "Wade can drive the boys home to get dry clothes. I'll ride with you, and they can meet us at the hospital with dry clothes for us."

"Sounds like a good plan," Wade added. "Come on, boys, lets go get dry." He looked over at Dixie. "Keys?"

"You sure you don't mind? I should have asked before I volunteered you for this."

"Dixie, come on. This is me you're talking to. If you need something, you don't have to ask."

She smiled and pressed her keys into his hand. "Thank you."

"You're welcome. I guess the boys know where to find dry clothes for you and Pops?"

"In our bedrooms. Just bring me some dry jeans, shirt, socks." She looked down at her soaked sneakers. "And shoes."

"We'll take care of it," he promised. "Come on, boys, lets go."

Wade was tempted to forgo dry clothes for himself. He wanted to take care of the boys and get dry clothes to Dixie and Pops as soon as possible, and going by his place would slow things down. But he knew that deliberately staying chilled, then walking into a hospital, notoriously brimming with enough germs, viruses and bacteria to choke a bull elephant, was nothing short of foolish for a transplant patient with little to no immune system.

He decided to swing by his place first and grab clothes to change into later. That would only keep everyone else waiting, including driving time, three minutes, max. Small towns definitely had their advantages.

He pulled up next to his front door and killed the engine. "Stay here, boys, I'll be right back. I'm going to run inside and get dry clothes."

"Can we come?" Tate asked. "We wanna see where you live."

"Okay, but we have to hurry. Your mom and Pops are waiting for us."

How odd, Wade thought a moment later as he unlocked his door and held it open, that he would be nervous over what Ben and Tate thought of his home. Or, what they thought was his home.

And how fitting that they were his first visitors.

Both boys made for the couch, where they plopped down, soaking-wet butts and all.

"Does anybody live here with you?" Ben wondered.

"No. Just me." He went directly to the dresser in his bedroom and scooped out shorts and socks, then, from the closet, jeans and a shirt and a dry pair of shoes. In the bathroom he grabbed a towel.

"Cool, man, you've got your own TV." Tate grabbed the remote and started pushing buttons.

The television came on at a blare.

"No time," Wade turned the set off. "We have to go."

He wouldn't have been surprised if they had dragged their feet, or darted off to the kitchen or bedroom or bathroom, anything to explore and delay. They were, after all, boys.

But they followed him out and climbed up into the SUV with no argument, squishing in their wet sneakers.

The rain had stopped. The sun streaked golden and rose from the western horizon. It looked odd, with the sky overhead still dark and gray.

The next stop was the McCormick residence, maybe four minutes away by car. He would have used one of the keys Dixie had given him, but the boys bolted ahead of him to the back door and dashed inside. The door had been unlocked.

He shook his head. He didn't care how small the town was. He doubted he would ever be able to deliberately leave the door to his home unlocked.

He followed the boys inside, pleased to note that they weren't dripping copious amounts of water on the floor. "Point me to your mom's room. I'll get her dry clothes while you two change."

"This way." Tate tugged his arm and led him through the kitchen to the hall. "That's Mom's room down there." He pointed to the right.

"Okay. You two change into dry clothes." Remembering his own boyhood, and a young boy's basic in-clinations, he added, "That means dry underwear, too."

A round of back-and-forth snickering and shoving was their response.

Wade stepped into Dixie's bedroom. He found the light switch on the wall next to the door and flipped it. Soft light flooded the room, gleaming along oak furniture, making the peach-colored coverlet and drapes glow with warmth. A woman's room, but one in which a man would not feel uncomfortable.

However, entering a woman's bedroom without her there to invite him left him feeling like a cross between a peeping Tom and a burglar. It didn't matter that she'd asked him to come there. He still felt odd. The sooner he could leave, the better.

But when he opened a dresser drawer and saw a neat stack of filmy, lace-edged bikini panties in shades from pale barely blue to touch-me-and-burn red, he suddenly found it hard to breathe, let alone move. He swallowed. Hard. And did his best not to visualize what Dixie might look like in a pair of these teasers and nothing else.

With a deep breath, he closed his eyes, grabbed a pair and shut the drawer.

Oh, hell. She would need a dry bra, too.

He opened another drawer and there they were, lacy bras to match the panties.

He looked at the scrap of fabric in his hand. Red. Okay. One red bra, to match. If his hand wasn't quite steady when he reached for it, well, that was to be expected, wasn't it? It had been a long time since he'd been anywhere near a woman's underwear. So to speak.

And this woman, in particular, was waiting, cold and wet and worried about Pops, for Wade to show up with dry clothes for her. "Get it in gear, mister," he muttered to himself.

In the closet he found jeans, a shirt and shoes.

Did she need socks?

Back to the dresser. Socks were in the bottom drawer on the right. He grabbed a pair.

Makeup. Should he take her makeup to her?

If he did, would she think that he thought she needed it?

If he didn't take her makeup, and she wanted it, would she think he was an unthinking jerk?

The underwear was one thing. She had to have dry underwear. But she was going to know he was in her underwear drawers. What was she going to think of that?

How was a man supposed to know what to do when it came to women and underwear and makeup?

Forget the makeup, he decided. He found the linen closet in the hall and grabbed a couple of towels for her and Pops.

"Boys? How are you doing?"

"We're ready." They bounded out of their room and met him in the hall.

"All right. Let's turn out the lights." He reached

into Dixie's bedroom and flipped the switch off, plunging the room into deep shadows. The sun had set. There was no twilight this far south. Once the sun set, it got dark quickly.

He wrapped Dixie's clothes in one of the towels and placed the bundle in the SUV. The evening air smelled of fresh rain.

"Now we need clothes for Pops."

"Come on." This time Ben took his arm. "We'll show you. Pops lives back here."

The boys led him along a narrow sidewalk that ran down the outside of the garage to a small apartment in the rear. This door, too, was unlocked.

The apartment was tiny but complete, with separate rooms for kitchen, living room, bedroom. The boys helped him pick out dry clothes and shoes for Pops, and they were on their way in a matter of minutes.

"Wade?" Ben's voice sounded small.

"Yes?"

"They said when our dad got hurt—"

Everything inside Wade stilled.

"—they took him to the hospital, but he died."

"I heard about that," Wade managed. "I'm sorry. It must be hard to lose your dad."

"Yeah, but that was a long time ago." The boy hesitated. "Is, is Pops gonna die?"

"No," Wade said emphatically. "Well, I mean someday, sure. Everybody dies eventually, right? But not tonight. Hopefully not for a long, long time. Pops just hurt his ankle, that's all."

"Honest?"

"Honest. I swear. We're almost there, so you can see for yourself."

Wade's prediction proved accurate. Pops had a sprained ankle. It was a bad sprain, according to Dr. Hoskins, but nothing was broken. Pops was *not* happy to be told to keep off that ankle for at least a couple of days, that he needed to stay home with that foot elevated. Pops wanted to argue that he had to work, but Dixie kissed him on the forehead and told him to hush. Oddly, he did.

Wade rode home from the hospital with the McCormicks so he could help Pops get settled in the man's apartment. Dixie would join Pops and Wade after she took the boys into the house, and they would talk about the diner.

Far off toward the east, thunder rumbled. The occasional shaft of lightning set the black clouds aglow. Overhead, stars popped out in the clear sky. Wet streets reflected streetlights, headlights, porch lights. The air smelled sweet, felt damp against the skin.

For the second time that night Wade entered the garage apartment behind Dixie's garage. At least this time he didn't feel like a trespasser as he held the door open for Pops to maneuver his way inside on his crutches.

"You want to sit in here or go straight to bed?" Wade asked.

"Bed, hell. I've got a twisted ankle, not terminal cancer."

Wade pursed his lips to keep from grinning. "Sorry. Just trying to help. Why don't I go scrounge around the kitchen for something to make an ice pack with. Unless you have a real ice pack around someplace?"

"Never had much need for one before."

"I'll see what I can come up with."

Wade searched the kitchen and came up with a plastic bag, the kind that zipped closed. He shook his head at the old-fashioned ice-cube trays in the freezer. He hadn't seen a refrigerator without an automatic ice maker in years.

Well, as long as he didn't count the one in his current apartment. Maybe it was a Texas thing. But, no, he recalled Dixie's kitchen clearly enough, and she had an automatic ice and water dispenser in her fridge.

He filled the bag with ice cubes, zipped it closed, then burped it a few times to get as much air out as possible. He pulled the dish towel off the cabinet doorknob next to the sink and considered his mission accomplished.

He carried the makeshift ice pack to the divan, where Pops sat with his foot propped on the coffee table. Wade draped the dish towel over the bandaged ankle, then carefully placed the bag of ice on top.

"How's that?"

"Fine. Thanks. Have a seat."

"You want any aspirin or anything?"

"No, but now that you mention it, I sure could use a beer. Get one for yourself while you're at it."

"You've got a deal."

"Sure was glad you were around tonight," Pops offered.

Wade opened two bottles of beer and gave one to Pops. With a sigh, he sat on the opposite end of the divan. "I was glad to help."

"She does too much," Pops said, looking older than Wade had ever seen him. "Has too much on her plate. Business, employees, mortgage, two young boys, an old man who can't manage his own two feet without tripping over them."

"I think if you asked her, she'd say those were good things. All of them. If I hadn't been there tonight, she would have handled everything just fine."

"Maybe, but we'd still be wet and cold without the dry clothes you brought."

"There is that."

"See? She needed you tonight. We all did. Which makes me want to ask just how long you plan on hanging around."

Wade took a sip of beer and leaned back to hide the fact that his heart started pounding. "So, are you asking?"

"She doesn't have a man to stand for her."

"Oh, yes, she does. She's got you," Wade said. "Don't sell yourself short, Pops."

"I'm an old man. I won't be around forever. And you didn't answer my question."

"I don't know how to answer it," Wade said honestly. "But I will tell you this. I can't explain yet, but neither Dixie nor her sons will ever want for anything, whether I stay or go, whether I live or die."

"Do tell. How in the hell do you plan to manage that? Does she know about any of this?"

Wade suddenly thought he knew what a tightrope walker must feel—one wrong step and, *kablooey.* "Not yet," he said. "And I'd appreciate if you wouldn't say anything until I've had a chance to talk to her about it."

"I knew there was something about you right from the beginning. Who are you?"

Wade met the old man's gaze squarely. "My name's Wade Harrison, I swear. I mean only good for Dixie and the boys. I would cut off my right arm before I would intentionally hurt them."

Pops studied him for a long moment. "What aren't you telling me?"

"Only what I can't." *Your grandson's heart beats in my chest.* "Not yet. Not until I find a way to explain to Dixie."

Again Pops studied him. "I guess I don't have any choice right now but to take you at your word."

"Thank you." The relief left him weak and shaky.

This man's opinion meant a great deal to him, and it had nothing to do with the man's relationship to McCormick.

"But I've got my eye on you, boy."

"Yes, sir."

"Now we'll shut up about it. I just heard the back door open. She's coming."

By the time Dixie joined Pops and Wade in the garage apartment, they were seated on the divan, sipping beer, both men with their feet propped on the coffee table. Two running shoes, one loafer, one set of bare toes peeking out from beneath a bag of ice. Her own legs were rubbery with the need to get off them and rest.

"I brought these," she said to Pops. "I'll put them in the freezer. You can use them after those cubes melt."

"Peas?" Pops eyed the bag skeptically. "You brought me a bag of frozen peas?"

"For your ankle." She crossed the room and put the peas in the freezer.

"Boys get settled down?" Pops asked.

"More or less." She took a beer from the fridge and opened it.

"Sit down," Pops said. "Before you fall down. Mercy, girl, you look worse than I do."

"Gee, thanks." She sank onto the easy chair facing the divan.

"Maybe you're the one who should stay home tomorrow." Pops laughed at his own joke.

Dixie smirked. "Somehow I don't think Wade would appreciate having to run the place by himself."

"You got that right," Wade said. "Even if I did, you'd lose all your business. I can scramble eggs and grill steaks and burgers outdoors. Otherwise, if it involves anything more complicated than a microwave, it's beyond my abilities."

"Don't worry about it." Pops waved away any concern. "I'll do the cooking tomorrow, same as I always do."

"But you can't," Dixie protested. "You heard the doctor."

"Ah, what does he know? I've got shirts older than him."

"Your shirts don't have a medical degree," she fired back. "You're staying home for the next two days with your foot propped up right where it is."

"Am not."

"Heaven help me, you sound just like one of the boys."

He grinned at her. "Do not."

She looked at Wade, who appeared to be trying very hard not to pay attention. "You see what I have to put up with?"

"Oh, no." He raised a hand in the air. "I'm not taking sides in this. Except to say that I agree, Pops, you need to stay home." And Wade knew as he said

the words just what it meant, how it felt, to let—no,
to be forced by circumstances beyond your control,
by the betrayal of your own body—to let someone
else take over your domain. It hurt like hell.

"Traitor."

"What can I say?" Wade offered a sympathetic
smile. "She signs my paycheck."

Pops sighed. "I guess every man has his price, but
I thought you were better than that."

"This is all very amusing," Dixie said, "but I need
to go call around and find someone to work tomorrow."

"Can you cook?" Wade asked.

"Of course, but not while I'm waiting tables."

"Why can't I wait tables?"

"You?" She stared openmouthed.

"You?" Pops looked thoughtful.

"Yes, me. I can wait tables. I mean, if you don't
try to make me wear a skirt."

Dixie had a sudden vision of Wade in a skirt, bare,
hairy legs sticking out. She burst into laughter.

"I'm glad you think it's funny," he muttered.

"Nah, don't worry." Pops slapped him on the
shoulder. "She can't make you wear no skirt, seeing
as how she never wears one herself."

"Are the two of you going to take this act on the
road?" Dixie asked. "If I cook and Wade waits tables,
who's going to wash dishes?"

Wade shrugged. "How long can we go without
running out?"

Pops cleared his throat. "I could—"

"No!" Dixie and Wade said in unison.

"You're staying home," Dixie stated.

"And that's that," Wade added. "Surely the two of us can manage for a while in the morning. If it looks like we won't make it on our own, you can call in help. Or maybe that man who came by looking for work will come back."

Pops squeezed one eye shut and peered at the two of them with the other. "It could work. If everybody hustles."

Dixie had to agree. It could work. "If business is light. I can't believe I'm hoping business will be light. Still, I guess we'll give it a try. And, Wade, I really appreciate this extra effort. We're all of us grateful for your help tonight."

"Hell, girl, don't go thanking him. He'll start thinking he's not one of the family, and I guess we've pretty much adopted him after tonight."

She smiled. "I guess you're right. He's ours."

She had no idea, Wade thought, just how true that was. At least, his heart was theirs. In more ways than one, if the emotions tumbling around inside him meant anything. But he was surprised, in view of their earlier conversation, that Pops would say so. Surprised, relieved and enormously pleased.

He had never known, he thought as he sat there and listened to the two of them talk about everyday things, laundry, the boys' homework, what it was to stand, if not on the outside, then right on the edge of something so...appealing, so perfect, to want it for himself, to forget for long hours at a time that it wasn't already his.

It. Them. The woman with her wit and resolve and generosity. The man with his wisdom and integrity. The boys. Oh, God, those boys.

They weren't his. He knew that. He hadn't come here to make them his. But now he wanted them. He wanted their mother. She hadn't been part of his plans at all, yet he felt that if he didn't get his hands—and his mouth—on her, and soon, he might go insane.

And now the tabloids knew he was missing from New York. His sister was right. They would find him. So he'd better get his act together, do whatever it was he was going to do about the memory of James Donald McCormick, and get the hell out of Dodge.

Was he going to tell Dixie he had her ex's heart? Was he going to tell her sons?

If he told anyone, it would have to be her. Then it would be her decision whether or not to let the boys know.

But first, he thought with a silent laugh, he had to turn himself into a waitress.

God, if his board of directors could see him now.

"You're smiling," Dixie said.

"What? Oh. Just relaxing. It's been a hectic evening. I bet Tate was disappointed about his game getting rained out."

"Yes, he was. And speaking of my sons, I better get back and check on them. They're supposed to be cleaning their rooms and getting ready for bath time." She pushed herself to her feet.

Wade rose, too. "I'll walk out with you. Good night, Pops. Enjoy your time off."

"Hmph."

"Can I do anything for you?" Dixie asked Pops. "Bring you anything?"

"I'll be fine, Dixie girl. You two skedaddle now so this old man can get his beauty rest."

"All right, then." She leaned down and kissed his cheek. "I'll be out in the morning to change your bandage before I leave for work."

"You will not. I'm a grown man. I can change my own bandage."

Dixie started to argue, but Wade took her arm and gave it a gentle but definite squeeze.

"We'll be going, then," Wade said. "Thanks for the beer."

Wade practically dragged Dixie outside and shut the door behind them.

"What was that for?" Dixie pulled free from his loose grasp.

"He needs to do something for himself. Being dependent on you, or anybody, makes him feel useless."

"Well, that's just nonsense," she retorted.

"Of course it is." Wade pulled her to a stop at the base of the steps to her back door. "He'll forget all about it tomorrow. He'll be dying for somebody to talk to, somebody to fuss over him, by the time you and the boys get home. But for tonight, he needs to be alone."

"What's he going to do, have a pity party?"

"That's it exactly. He needs to mope around and feel sorry for himself and gripe about feeling useless."

She smiled up at him. "How did you come to know him so well?"

"He's my grandfather all over again. If I didn't know better I'd swear they were twins. Not physically, but in every other way."

"Wade…" She placed a hand on his arm.

That was all the invitation Wade needed. "Dixie." He pulled her to his chest and slipped his arms around her. "You're tired."

She wrapped her arms around his neck and pulled his face toward hers. "Not that tired."

"Oh, good." He didn't so much kiss her as drink her in. As if he'd just spent forty days and nights in the desert, and she was his oasis. She tasted sweet and dark, the way a woman should. She smelled the same way.

He ran his hands up her back and down again. He wanted to pull her inside, so she was a part of him for real instead of only in his yearnings.

"I can't get enough of you," he murmured against her lips.

Dixie felt herself melt into him, her bones, her

muscles. "Feel free," she whispered between nibbles, "to keep trying until you do."

"That could take a while." His tongue traced her bottom lip.

Dixie shivered. Deep down inside, heat pulsed. "I've got plenty of time."

"Oh, good." And he drank her up again.

She reveled in his kiss. Her fingers found their way into his thick, short hair. Against her abdomen, she felt…

It was the snickering from the back door that broke the kiss.

"Told ya they were smooching," Ben whispered.

"Ooh, yuk," Tate answered. "A lip-lock. Cooties."

Wade dropped his forehead against hers. "Time just ran out."

"The story of my life."

"Why don't you guys go watch TV while I finish kissing your mama?"

More snickers, then the back door squeaked shut.

"There." He settled her hips against his. "Now, where were we? Oh, I remember. I was chasing cooties, just about…here." He buried his lips in her neck.

She shuddered against him. "No fair. I have to go in." Her head fell back to give him better access. "In a minute. Oh, yes. Right…there. I'll go in in a minute."

In fact, it was several minutes before she went in, and even then she didn't walk so much as she floated. Or, it felt that way to her.

Before closing the door, she turned and looked back. He was still standing there. "Wade?"

"Yeah?"

"Thank you."

"You're welcome. I've always thought of myself as a good kisser, but most women don't actually say thanks."

"Oh, ha-ha. Get to work thirty minutes before opening tomorrow. We'll see how well your sense of humor stands up to waiting on tables."

When she closed the door, Wade finally turned to go. He was halfway home before he realized he was still smiling.

Chapter Seven

The first customer entered the diner less than a minute after Dixie told Wade to unlock the door. Wade was still putting the keys away when the door opened.

Having spent nearly all his time in the diner hidden away in the kitchen, Wade did not know more than a scant few of their customers, and even then, he didn't know anyone's name. He wasn't going to be able to relate to people the way Dixie did, with a familiar ease. He would have to make up for it with that charm his mother claimed he had in abundance.

This first customer was an elderly woman in a

black-and-white flowered dress, a white pillbox hat and, of all things, white, wrist-length cotton gloves.

"Good morning," Wade called out from behind the counter. "Just sit anywhere and I'll be right with you."

She eyed him suspiciously and sat near the front. Table two.

Wade filled a water glass with ice and water and grabbed a menu. At her table, he presented them to her.

"Young man, who are you and where is Dixie?"

"Ma'am." He gave her a slight bow. "Dixie is doing the cooking this morning. I'm Wade."

She tapped her fingers on the plastic-coated menu and eyed him much the same way his third grade teacher had when he was about to get a lecture on deportment.

Then her eyes widened. "You're Dixie's new dishwasher, aren't you?"

"Yes, ma'am. Wade Harrison. May I get you some coffee or tea while you decide what you want for breakfast?"

"We'll get to that. Tell me why Dixie is in the kitchen. Where is Pops?"

Small town, Wade thought. Everyone either knew everything about your business, or they were trying their damnedest to find out. Maybe he didn't mind that as much as he thought he would. The lady was looking out for Dixie. He had to appreciate that.

"Pops slipped and sprained his ankle in the rain

last night, bad enough to have the doctor tell him to stay home and prop it up for a couple of days."

"Why, that poor man. I'll have to take him a casserole this afternoon. You tell Dixie not to worry about feeding him tonight. It will be taken care of."

"Yes, ma'am. I'm sure Pops will appreciate it."

"Well, my goodness gracious, where are my manners? You can't very well tell her I'm taking over a casserole if you don't know my name, now, can you? Silly me. My name is Ima Trotter, and yes, I've heard all the jokes, so don't waste your time making fun of my name. I worked at the Tribute Post Office from 1952 to 1990. Was postmaster the last thirty years of that. I am now retired."

Wade cocked his head. "Postmaster, not postmistress?"

"Technically, postmistress. However, when you hear the word mistress, young man, what is the first thing you think of?"

"Ah, yes." Wade nodded sagely. "I see what you mean."

"Precisely. Now, I believe I shall accept your offer of coffee while I decide what to eat." She opened her menu and peered at it through the bottoms of her thick bifocals.

"Yes, ma'am. One coffee, coming up. Do you take cream with that?"

"No, thank you."

While Wade picked up a coffee mug and the coffeepot, the boys came into the dining room. Bored, probably, Wade thought. He hadn't seen any school books, so they wouldn't have homework to occupy them.

"Hey, Miz Trotter," Ben said.

"Good morning," the woman said. "How are two of my favorite young men this fine morning?"

"We're okay," Ben said.

"But Pops hurt his ankle, so he had to stay home," Tate told her.

"So I heard. I'm sure he's not happy about that."

"No, ma'am," Tate said. "He even used bad words."

"He did? My, my. I'll have to have a serious talk with him, don't you think?"

"I don't know," Tate said. "Mom pretty much let him have it."

Wade did his best not to laugh as he placed the mug on the table before her and filled it with coffee. "Do you know what you want yet, or do you need more time?"

The boys snickered. "How do you like our new waitress?"

Miz Trotter smiled at the joke.

Wade scowled and shook his fist in the air. "You want to be nice to the person who'll be bringing your breakfast to you."

"Whoops." Ben saluted.

Tate copied the gesture. "Yes, sir. This is us being nice."

"Shoo. Go work on your multiplication tables."

"No way! We don't have any homework."

"So you can't get better at what you barely know unless somebody forces you? Don't you practice batting, even if there's no game?"

"But that's *baseball*," Ben said indignantly, "not *multiplication*."

"How do you figure out a player's earned-run average?"

"You read it in the paper or wait for the announcer at the game to tell you what it is."

"What if it's your ERA. How do you know the announcer got it right?"

"Neither one of us is a pitcher, so we can't have an ERA."

"So what? You've got at least one pitcher on your team. Well," Wade added, ruffling Tate's hair. "You will have next year."

He had them thinking now. On the way back to their booth in the banquet room they made a bet as to who could figure out an ERA first.

"That was nicely done," Miz Trotter said.

"Thanks," he said. "They're really something, aren't they?"

"That they are. It was a real shame about their father. He might not have had much ambition, unless it was for the rodeo, but that Jimmy Don did dearly love his sons. Now, as for my breakfast, I'll have two eggs over easy with bacon, and on a separate plate, a pecan waffle with heated syrup. And I'll take a small orange juice with that."

"Yes, ma'am." Wade wrote as fast as he could on his order pad. By the time he got the order turned in to Dixie she had the boys' breakfast ready. While he delivered those, three more customers entered the diner.

Time to get to work, in earnest.

During the course of the day Wade solemnly and repeatedly vowed to be considerably more generous with his tips in the future. God, what a job.

Everyone was nice to him, cut him plenty of slack when he didn't do things just the way Dixie would have, or if he got an order wrong, which, thankfully, he only did twice.

He and Dixie worked well together, if he did say so himself. She seemed to have no trouble figuring out what he wrote, only having to ask him a couple of questions. When she called that an order was ready, she told him if any side garnishes needed to be added, and he added them himself.

Around 10:30 a.m. there was a lull, with the breakfast crowd cleared out and the lunch crowd not yet there. They caught a breather. Wade finished busing the last of the tables, then rinsed off a load of dishes and started them through the dishwasher.

"I could have done that," Dixie protested.

"So could I. So I did. How are you holding up back here?"

"I was going to ask you the same question." She pressed her hands to the small of her back and arched. "Standing in one place is harder than walking around all day."

"Here." He wiped his hands on a towel, then pushed her hands away and gripped her waist.

"What are you doing?"

"Be still." With his thumbs, he dug into the knotted muscles on either side of her spine.

"Oh." Then she let out a long, low moan. "Oh, yeah. That feels…wonderful."

"At Dixie's Diner, we aim to please. Mmm. You smell…delicious."

Dixie chuckled. "You must be hungry. I smell like bacon. Oh, God, that feels good. We should open a massage parlor in the back room and put you to work in there. With those hands of yours, we'd both make a fortune."

"You think so?" He moved up her back and went to work on her shoulders. "You're tight up here." He massaged the back of her neck and up into her scalp. Her head fell back until he was supporting its weight in his hands.

"I'm not used to slaving over a hot stove all morning."

"I'd offer to trade jobs with you, but so far I don't think we've done any permanent damage to your business or your clientele. If I cook, I don't think we'll be able to say the same. That'd be a shame, because so far I like your clientele."

"Yeah, I know. You just like it better out front where you can flirt with all the ladies."

"We're getting to know each other," he said cryptically. "Speaking of ladies," he added, "I'm supposed to tell you that Miz Ima Don't-Make-Fun-of-My-Name Trotter will be taking a casserole to Pops this afternoon, so you're not to worry about him sitting home all alone and starving to death."

"My, my," Dixie said. "You really are getting to know the ladies, aren't you?"

He trailed his fingers down her back, then poked them in her ribs. She flinched, jerked away and shrieked with laughter.

"Now I know where Tate gets his ticklishness from."

"Watch it, buster."

Laughing, he let her go. "I'll have you know that I'm also getting to know the men, too." He shook his head as if in sorrow. "I'm sorry to say, they don't like me as well as the ladies do."

"Is that so?" She held a spatula out to ward him off as she circled around him to get back to the grill.

"Yes, indeed. How was it the man from the hardware store, Frank, I think he said his name was, put it? Something about…oh, yes. My butt's not as cute as yours."

Dixie's eyes widened in outrage. "Frank Schmidt's been ogling my butt?"

"I have to tell you, being told I'm not as attractive as someone else hurt my feelings."

"Frank Schmidt," she screeched toward the open order window, "has been looking at my *butt?* Where is that dirty old man?" She started toward the door, spatula held aloft like a bat. "Is he still here?"

Wade was laughing so hard he barely caught her before she stormed out into the dining room to wreak havoc on sixty-year-old Frank Schmidt.

"Now, hold on," he told her, still laughing. "Take it easy. You can't go out there and beat up a paying customer. Besides, the poor guy's half-blind, anyway."

The bell over the front door dinged, announcing the arrival of a new customer.

"Hmph." Dixie sniffed and gave him a shove. "Back to work, waitress."

If breakfast had been busy, lunch sent Wade and Dixie reeling. A good dozen people came in just for coffee or a slice of pie, so they could check out the new "waitress" they'd heard about from friends who'd been in for breakfast.

That part of the lunch trade was all in good fun, but it sure added extra work for Wade, serving drinks, refilling them, cleaning up the tables afterward.

But the real lunch trade, the people who came in for a meal, was slightly more work than the breakfast crowd. At lunch the orders were more varied and sometimes trickier. Everyone wanted substitutions. Mustard instead of mayonnaise, toasted rather than plain. Baked potato instead of fries. Oops. No baked potatoes until after five.

It was like running a marathon. He guessed. He'd never run a marathon. But he'd gone several miles at a stretch, and this was damn near as taxing.

But he was gratified by everyone's concern for Dixie's whereabouts and Pops's injury.

At the same time, he knew the clock was ticking. Washing dishes kept him pretty much hidden from most of the customers. Now he was out among them, talking to them, serving them their food. It wasn't out of the realm of possibility that the next person through that door would recognize him.

He had to tell Dixie the truth, and soon. Or decide not to tell her at all.

Telling her would presume that she wanted to know. It would surely dredge up old sorrow over Jimmy Don's death. Yet not telling her at all felt sneaky and underhanded and somehow dishonest.

And there was still the matter of leaving behind some way for Ben and Tate to know that their father was a hero.

To top it all off, when he left, Dixie was going to have to hire a new dishwasher.

"You're not Dixie," the man at table three said when Wade took him a menu and glass of ice water. "And I'll bet you've been hearing that all day."

Wade smiled. "That I have. I'm Wade, the dish-washer," he explained for what must have been the zillionth time. "Pops is home with his sprained ankle propped up, and Dixie's manning the stove. That leaves me to be your server."

"I'd heard Dixie had hired someone from out of town. That must be you."

"There's nothing wrong with the grapevine in this town."

"Not a thing. Welcome to Tribute." The man stuck out his hand for a shake. "I'm Bill Gray, with the *Tribute Banner.*"

Wade shook his hand and smiled. "William Henley Gray. I recognize your name. That was an interesting editorial last week about Homeland Security. You should send a copy of it to your U.S. senators and representatives to let them know how you feel, and that you're not the only one who feels that way."

A light gleamed in Bill Gray's eyes. "Did that very thing last week." He tilted his head and narrowed his eyes. "Forgive me, but could we have met somewhere before? You look familiar."

Here it comes, Wade thought, tensing. The end of his anonymity. But he spoke the truth when he answered. "I've been around for a couple of weeks. I walk around town a lot, for exercise. Go to some of the Little League games to watch Dixie's kids play. Maybe we've run into each other. I'll be back in a couple of minutes to take your order. Unless you already know what you want?"

Gray studied him a moment longer, then shook his head. "It'll come to me, where I've seen you before."

I hope not, Wade thought, trying not to let his wariness show.

"As for my order," Gray said, "I'll have the grilled chicken salad with ranch dressing and Texas toast. And iced tea."

"I'll have that out to you in a few minutes."

By two o'clock the bulk of the lunch crowd was gone. Wade stood in the front window, hands on his hips and shook his head. By all rights there should be a huge crowd out there, their backs to him as they dispersed around town after their lunch at Dixie's Diner.

Not a pedestrian in sight, and very few cars.

Oh, look, an old gray panel truck pulled in at the gas station across the street. Traffic!

He hoped, and was ashamed of himself for it, that they didn't want to eat.

He was turning back to face all the dirty dishes scattered over nearly every table, when a man stepped out of the panel truck. It was the man who had come in the other day looking for work.

Here, then, might be the answer to one of his dilemmas.

He started to yell to Dixie that he would be right back, but there were still two customers, one at table six finishing off the last of his pecan pie, and the other at booth four drinking coffee and working a crossword puzzle.

Wade stuck his head in the kitchen. "That man who was looking for a job the other day is across the street. Do you want me to run over there and see if he's interested in helping us out?"

With her forearm, she wiped the perspiration off her brow and peered through the order window at the tables beyond. At the mess beyond. Then she looked around the kitchen, which looked as if a Texas tornado had struck.

"Oh, yeah," she agreed. "Just be sure and tell him it's temporary, okay? I wouldn't want to get his hopes up."

"Gotcha."

Feeling guilty as sin, because he knew she was going to need permanent help soon, Wade headed for the front door. On his way out, he called to the two customers, "I'll be right back. If you need anything, Dixie's in the kitchen."

He felt foolish looking both ways for traffic on a street that saw maybe a dozen cars an hour. Hell, compared to Manhattan, Main Street in Tribute, Texas, was a vacant field. Still, he would feel even more foolish to step out and get creamed by a house-wife on her way to the grocery store. So, he looked both ways. Then dashed across the street.

The man pumping gas into the panel truck saw

him coming and suddenly looked uneasy, darting his eyes back and forth, turning slightly away as if he hadn't seen Wade.

Illegal, Wade guessed. No green card.

They could sort that out later. After the dishes were washed.

"Pardon me, sir, but you came into the café the other day looking for work, didn't you?"

"*Sí.* I was looking for work there."

"Do you still need work?"

"Me? No, *señor,* I am now employed at the construction company down the street. I start there today."

"Oh, well, good for you. The pay's a lot better there, I'm sure."

"You need help, *señor?*"

"Yes, we need help. Thanks for—"

"*Señor,* excuse, *por favor.* My son, he is nineteen. He needs work."

Wade's hopes perked up. "Where is he?"

The man banged on the side of the truck and yelled in Spanish for his son to come out. A moment later the back door of the van opened and a medium-height young man with the coal-black hair and dark brown eyes of his father stepped out.

"*¿Sí, padre?*"

"This man, he has work for you."

"For me?" The boy's eyes lit up with excitement. "What kind of work?" he asked Wade.

"Across the street, at the diner. Busing tables,

washing dishes, pushing the occasional mop or broom. Are you interested?"

"Yes, I am interested. When can I start?"

"Right now, if you want. You'll only work a few hours today, but tomorrow we'll need you all day."

The teenager looked at his father. The man eyed Wade a long moment, then glanced at the diner. "Are you the boss?" the man asked.

"No. The boss is the woman you spoke with the other day. Dixie McCormick."

"I remember. She seemed like a nice lady."

"She's a very nice lady."

Finally the man gave the nod to his son. "You go straight back to our rooms when you're finished for the day. *Tu madre,* she will be looking for you."

"Yes, sir." The boy turned to Wade. "I am ready now."

"Then let's go."

Dixie gathered the potatoes and carrots she would need for the roast she was going to put in the oven before she left. Then she took out a clove of garlic and instant onion flakes. This was one of the few instances when the dried worked better than the fresh. She placed everything in the roasting pan and set it aside. It was too early to start cooking dinner.

As long as this lull in business held, she would clean up after herself. She had spilled flour all over the cutting board and the floor, and then there was the splattered grease. She looked around and frowned. The kitchen never looked this messy when Pops cooked.

But if she told him that, his head would swell so big he wouldn't be able to wear that twenty-year-old Stetson he refused to replace.

And speaking of cleaning up, how long was Wade going to be gone? She checked her watch.

Okay, he'd been gone two minutes. It did not please her to realize that she could actually *feel* when he was near and when he wasn't. What did that mean?

The bell over the door dinged. She didn't need to hear his voice to know it was him. Her internal radar—her Wade detector, as Pops put it—told her it was him. A moment later he more or less exploded into the kitchen with a young Hispanic man in tow.

"Dixie McCormick, meet your new dishwasher, Miguel Ortega. His father is the man who came in the other day, but he's working for a construction company now. Miguel was looking for work, too, so, here he is."

"Miguel," she said, extending her hand. "Welcome." He shook her hand with a combination of shyness and eagerness. "I guess Wade told you what we need?"

"He told me, yes."

"And you're okay with that?"

He nodded with his entire upper body. Almost a deferential bow. "Yes, ma'am. I have bussed tables and washed dishes before. I know what to do."

"Excellent," she said, relieved, hoping he was telling the truth.

"And now," Wade said, taking Miguel by the arm, "I'm going to show him around."

Dixie started to ask if Wade had told the boy the work was only temporary, but he must have. He knew he himself would go back to washing dishes when Pops came back.

It was too late to ask, anyway, as Wade had already ushered Miguel out the door and had him bussing tables.

She shrugged and used the edge of her spatula to scrape the gunk off the griddle. If a little voice in the back of her mind recalled that her first thought when she met Wade was that he hadn't looked as if he'd needed a job—especially not manual labor for minimum wage, and that if she hired him he wouldn't stay a week—she ignored it.

She'd been wrong. He'd stayed two weeks and counting. It could be time was running out for her.

Oh, now, wasn't that a telling thought? Time was running out for *her?* For her to what? She doubted that hiring a new dishwasher to replace Wade was what her unconscious mind was concerned about. No, her unconscious mind was concerned mainly with her family and, in this case, her personal happiness. Which meant that her tiny little pea brain had quite possibly decided that her personal happiness rested on whether Wade stayed or left.

And that was just bull hockey. She scrubbed harder on the griddle. Since when did her happiness, personal, superficial or otherwise, have anything to do with any man?

Since Wade Harrison.

"Oh, shut up."

"Okay, but I didn't say anything."

The voice—Wade's voice—startled her so much she shrieked and whirled, flinging the greasy crud of more than a dozen hamburgers from the end of her spatula. The gunk sailed through the air, arcing gracefully yet with serious force, straight into Wade's face.

"Oh!" She covered her mouth with her hands, but she couldn't quite squelch the bark of laughter at the look of shock on his face. "I…am so…" She tried to swallow, but another laugh escaped. "…sorry."

Wade wiped a hand down his face, then stared at the greasy mess that came off.

"Really," Dixie said. "I am…truly…sorry." *Snicker.*

He looked at her sadly. "So am I."

"You are?"

"I am."

"For what?"

"For this." He stepped forward and rubbed his gooey hand across her face.

"Wade!"

He smiled benignly. "Yes?"

"I can't believe you did that!"

"Actually, neither can I." He frowned and shook

his head. "I guess you bring out the teenager in me." *In more ways than one,* he thought, feeling the heated stirring in his blood at simply being near her. "It wasn't very gentlemanly of me."

"No, it wasn't," she said. "But I can't blame you. I would have done the same."

"You must have really been concentrating when I came in," he said.

"I was cleaning the griddle. How's Miguel doing?"

"Great. In fact, here he is now."

It took no more than a couple of minutes for Wade to show Miguel how to run the dishwasher. It turned out that he'd worked one similar to it at a previous job.

Oh, yeah, Wade thought, Dixie was going to want to keep this kid. All Wade had to do was break it to her that she needed to.

"Dix?" He moved toward her so they could have at least the appearance of privacy.

"What?"

"You know I take a lot of walks around town, right?"

"So I've heard."

"If I came by your house tonight, would you walk with me? Just the two of us?"

Dixie's mouth went dry while her palms grew damp. It was just a walk, she told herself. He wasn't asking her on a date. That her heart should suddenly race was just plain crazy. But she wanted to go. She wanted to take a walk with Wade.

"Okay," she managed. "About seven?"

"Great." His smile turned her knees weak. "I'll see you then."

She gave him a look from the corner of her eye. "How far are you going to make me walk?"

"Don't worry. Not too far. Just far enough to give us time to talk."

Chapter Eight

That evening Dixie looked around her dinner table and felt her heart swell. She was so lucky to have her family gathered around her every night. Pops's accident last night served to remind her never to take her life and the people she loved for granted.

"So, Pops, how was Miz Ima and her casserole?" she asked.

A deep red flush stole slowly up his cheeks. He scowled at her.

Dixie hooted with laughter. "Boys, I think Miz Trotter is sweet on Pops."

"You mean, like, boy-girl sweet on?" Ben asked, alarmed at the idea.

"Exactly."

"Eww, yuck," Tate said.

"My sentiments exactly," Pops muttered.

"Shame," Dixie said, laughing. "You've had a thing for her for twenty years."

The boys spent the next few minutes making gagging sounds.

They had yet to learn the value of girls.

"Have not," Pops protested. "Why, she's a good six months older than me."

"You know what they say about older women," Dixie teased.

"Oh, hush, you." The red blush now reached the tops of his ears.

"All right, all right," she conceded. "How's your ankle feeling?"

"Sore and swollen," he admitted tersely.

"You're still bent out of shape that I hired another dishwasher," she accused.

"What are you going to do with him when I come back to work? That's what I'd like to know."

So would Dixie, but she was afraid she would have her answer to that when Wade got there. "We'll see. But one thing to keep in mind, we both knew Wade wouldn't stay long."

Pops shot a look toward the boys, but they were still making gagging noises and hadn't heard Dixie's comment. She was grateful for that. Both boys worshiped Wade.

Dammit, she'd been doing fine keeping him out

of her mind until now. She feared she knew what he was going to say to her when they took their walk. He was going to say he was quitting. Leaving town. And she dreaded it. Her stomach tried to tie itself in a knot at the idea. The thought of never seeing him again created a yawning, empty hole inside her.

That stunned her. She knew she was attracted to him, that she liked him, even cared for him. Wanted him. But she hadn't realized that she was falling in love.

Oh, God, please, no. She could not, would not fall in love with a drifter. She would not fall in love with a man she had to support. Not again.

Yet hadn't she always thought that Wade came from money? Maybe he did. Maybe he was going back to it.

All this speculation was pointless. She glanced at the clock on the wall and noted that he would be there in forty-five minutes. She still had to clean the kitchen and get the boys and Pops to go to Pops's apartment.

How odd was it that she'd never asked to have the house to herself before?

She didn't care for what that said about the state of her love life. What it said was that she didn't have one.

Before Wade came clean to Dixie there was something he had to do. Something vitally important that he'd been putting off.

With directions from a man at the gas station, Wade drove beyond the south edge of town and up a small wooded hill. At the top the woods gave way to the ultimate tribute: the town cemetery.

It wasn't a very large cemetery, but when he climbed from the car he found the area quiet. A peaceful stillness lay over it. If a man's remains had to be planted in the ground for eternity, this was a good spot.

Having no idea where McCormick might be, he started walking the rows, reading the headstones. Some dated back to 1850 and earlier. Now and then a shrub hugged a marker. There was a scattering of flowers here, small American flags there. One grave was as recent as last week, the seams of the sod still visible where the grass had yet to knit together. A huge bouquet of tiny pink rosebuds rested beneath the headstone. He noted that it was for a two-year-old child. He couldn't imagine the pain of the parents, or the loss to the world of a young life cut short. Who knew what that child might have become if she'd had the chance?

Before the wave of sadness rolled completely over him, he moved away and walked faster.

It took him ten minutes to find what he was looking for. Several McCormick family members from the past eighty years occupied a section near the center of the cemetery by a gnarled cedar tree. On the outer edge of that section he found him. James Donald McCormick. Beloved father, son and grandson.

Gooseflesh rose across Wade's neck and down his arms. His heart paused, then raced.

"Hel—" Wade's voice caught. He cleared his throat and tried again. "Hello. I guess you know who I am. I got your heart."

He stopped, looked up at the deepening blue sky. Not a cloud in sight. "It seems odd to come here and talk to you. I feel like I've been carrying you around inside me for the past two years. And I have been, haven't I? I'm sorry you died, but by signing that organ donation card, well, you saved my life. I wouldn't have made it another day, and that's the truth."

He paused and looked around. It occurred to him that if someone heard him talking, they might think he was off his rocker. But then, people often talked to departed loved ones at gravesides, so who cared?

"You probably know I came here to check on your sons. It seemed as if that's what you wanted me to do. God, they're so alive, so…I don't know, perfect? I can't find the words. But I know why you loved them so much. They just reach right inside a man and fill his heart. Your heart."

He looked around again, because he had a confession to make that he'd just as soon no one overheard. He was still alone.

"I've already set up a college fund for each of the boys. I haven't figured out what else to do to make sure they never want for anything, but you can rest now, because I'll see to their future for you. I came here out of gratitude to you. I'm still here two weeks later out of love for them.

"I swear, I did not come here to hit on your ex-wife. I came for Ben and Tate. But she is quite a woman, your Dixie.

"Pops misses you, but he's doing all right…except for that fall he took at the game. But the damage is temporary. I'm still trying to find a way to make sure not only your sons, but everybody in town, knows what you did for not only me but the other people whose lives you saved or made livable again. I want people to be proud, to say, 'I knew him. He was the best.' I'll figure it out. But right now I've got to go explain to your ex-wife who I really am and why I'm here. If I don't find the right words, I might end up right next to you." He smiled. "I'd be proud to sleep next to you for eternity. Thank you, Jimmy Don. Thank you for my life."

It was a new concept for the McCormick men, that Mom should want the house to herself at a time of her own choosing.

Pops thought it was a fine, fine idea, except he feared Wade was going to tell her he was moving on.

Ben and Tate didn't get it. What could their mother possibly want to do that she couldn't do with them there? They frowned and scratched their heads, but Pops mentioned popcorn and a baseball movie on DVD. That was the end of their thoughts about Mom.

Dixie didn't know whether to be hurt or glad that they could forget about her so easily. She shook her head and watched them race across the yard toward the apartment ahead of Pops, who had to go slowly because of his crutches.

At last. Silence!

Except for the TV, which the boys had left on. Local news was over and one of those entertainment magazines was on. Nothing but gossip, Dixie thought with a shake of her head. She started across the living room to turn it off, but the picture on the screen, and then the accompanying audio, nailed her feet to the floor.

"One of the country's richest, most eligible bachelors seems to be missing in action. Media and entertainment mogul Wade Harrison hasn't been seen at any of his usual haunts for a couple of weeks now. No one at Harrison Corporation, where he served as CEO until his heart surgery two years ago and where he still sits on the board of directors, will comment on his whereabouts, but he was not at the Broadway opening last night starring his good friend Tom Cruise, and friends say it would take something major for him to miss Tom's Broadway debut. Hmm. Has anyone seen Wade Harrison lately? If you have, send us an e-mail here at the show."

The picture on the screen was of the dishwasher at Dixie's Diner in Tribute, Texas, but instead of jeans and a T-shirt, he was wearing a tux and a thousand-watt smile.

Dixie trembled with warring emotions. Fury, that Wade had failed to tell her who he really was. Humiliation at being duped. A gaping sense of loss for the man she'd thought she was falling for. A man who obviously didn't exist.

How *could* he? Damn him. "Wait until I get my hands on you, you rotten, no-good, lying son of a—" No one was allowed to swear in her house. She figured since she made the rule, she should abide by it.

But, oh, she could think of quite a few four-letter words to call him.

Outside, a shadow crossed her front window. She slapped the Off button on the TV just as a knock rattled the door.

It was Wade.

Oh, God. What was she going to say to him? She gnawed on her lip and paced the floor. Should she play dumb and see if he confessed? Maybe this was what he wanted to talk to her about.

Should she confront him with what she knew rather than give him a chance to tell her first?

Should she simply open the door and punch him in the mouth?

Yes. She liked that last one the best. Too bad she wouldn't do it.

He knocked again.

With a deep breath, she opened the door.

"Hi," he said, stepping inside with a smile.

"I'm glad you came," she said curtly. "If you'll wait here a minute, I'll get my checkbook and give you your final pay. Then you can be on your way."

Wade shook his head as if trying to clear water from his ear. "On my way?" He gave a brief laugh. "Are you firing me?"

She gave a jerky toss of her head. "You're here to tell me you're quitting, aren't you?"

Wade eyed her carefully. Something was going on here, something he didn't think he liked. She was really ticked off. At him, apparently.

"What's going on?" he asked carefully.

"What's going on, Mr. Bigshot Media Mogul, is that you've been playing me for a fool from the minute you walked into the diner that first day."

Wade hung his head and stared at the toes of his sneakers. She'd found out. Maybe not everything, but enough to make her angry.

"You can't even bother to deny it, can you?"

At the disgust in her voice, he snapped his head up. "What, that I came here to make a fool out of you? I do deny it. I flatly deny it. Yes, I wanted you to walk with me tonight because I had something to tell you. Obviously you've already heard at least part of it. Or someone else's version of it. Are you interested in hearing what I have to say?"

She turned her shoulder to him. "Not particularly."

"Well, that's too bad. What I have to say doesn't

concern only you. It concerns other people, too, so you don't get to make the decision to jump to conclusions and refuse to hear the truth."

"Me?" She cried in mock surprise. "Have a say in what goes on around here? Heaven forbid. Apparently, you're the one running this little farce. So, what was it, Wade, did you get bored in New York and decide to come down here to Texas for a little amusement?"

He leaned in close to her and kept his voice quiet. "If I was looking for amusement, I damn sure wouldn't be washing your dishes."

She folded her arms across her chest and glared at him. "Well, you've got me there. Why *are* you washing my dishes?"

Wade let out a long breath and rubbed the back of his neck. "It's a long story, and you have to let me tell it my way. Can we sit down, please? If you don't believe anything else tonight, Dixie, please believe that I never meant to deceive you or cause you trouble."

"Yeah. Right. Sit. I'm having iced tea. You want some?"

"Yes, please. But you don't have to wait on me."

"I'm not waiting on you. I'm keeping you out of my kitchen. Now, sit. Please."

"Yes, ma'am."

She rolled her eyes and stomped off to the kitchen.

If she was offering him tea, Wade figured that meant she was willing to listen. He took a seat on the sofa and wondered what she'd heard about him and where she'd heard it.

In the kitchen, ice cubes crashed into glasses. Liquid splashed. Then she was back, handing him a glass of iced tea.

"Here," she snapped.

"Thank you."

"Skip the pleasantries," she said. "Why are you here? Wait. Let me rephrase that. Why are you in Tribute, why are you working for me and why are you in my house right now?"

"Those are all fair questions," he began.

"Then answer them." There was no *please* this time as she sat on the easy chair facing him.

"I will, but I have to start a little farther back than that. I'm going to tell you a story."

"I don't want a damn story." She started to get up.

"Just stay put and give me a minute. The story's important. It will answer your questions."

"Then get to it."

Wade took a deep breath. "My family owns Harrison Corporation. Newspapers, magazines, movie theaters, video and DVD rental companies and a few other odds and ends in the news and entertainment field."

"So I heard."

"Where?"

"On TV, not thirty seconds before you got here. You are, in essence, missing in action from high society. Lucky me. I found you."

"Well, neither of my two older sisters was interested in running the corporation. They preferred their own individual arms of the company. And my father wanted to retire. So by the time I was twenty-seven, I was Harrison's CEO. Dad still sat as chairman of the board, but I handled the day-to-day business of running the company. I was responsible for our bottom line, I was the one who had to face the shareholders at the annual meeting if revenues fell below projections."

"A little young, weren't you?"

"By some standards, yes. But I ate, drank and slept the company while I was still in the womb. I was ready for the job and the responsibilities, and I did a damn good job of it, if I do say so myself."

"But?"

"But. Oh, yes, there's a but. It came one day in the spring of my twenty-ninth year. I collapsed on the racquetball court. To make a long story short, it turned out that sometime in my oh-so-proper youth, I had contracted an infection that got into my heart and did permanent damage that went undetected until the day I collapsed. Every day after that I went further and further downhill. I was dying."

Dixie paled. "My God, Wade. I had no idea."

"Of course you didn't. Why should you? The only thing that would save my life was a heart transplant. They put me on the list, but there are a lot more people waiting than there are donors."

"I assume you finally got a donor."

"At the very last possible minute. I wasn't going to make it through the night, and I knew it. Mom and Dad and the girls were there with me. It was just about the most grim atmosphere you can imagine. Then, a miracle happened. Somebody…had an accident. It's terrible to call that a miracle. It wasn't a miracle for him. But he was dead whether I got his heart or not, so I call it a miracle that I got his heart."

Dixie's own heart was thundering in her chest. "That's the scar I've seen just below your throat."

"Yes, but you've only seen the tip. It goes all the way down to my navel."

"Oh, my God, Wade. A heart transplant. That's just…like you said. It's a miracle you're even alive. But how did you end up here?"

Wade stared at the floor a moment, then briefly closed his eyes before facing her. "When I woke up after my transplant surgery, the first words I said were, 'Hug my two best boys for me.'"

Dixie quivered. *"What?"*

"You recognize those words?" he asked quietly.

Dixie felt suddenly light-headed. "No. *No.*"

But she did, and they both knew it.

"They call it cellular memory," Wade told her quietly. "But the only people who believe in it are transplant patients. Medical science doesn't put much stock in it. But I met a woman who woke up from her transplant surgery and asked for a beer.

She had always hated beer, but suddenly she wanted one. Turns out her donor was a big-time beer drinker. A man who received cornea transplants claimed he recognized his donor's wife on the street, when he had no idea who his donor or the man's wife were."

Dixie listened to what he was saying carefully. She drew in a breath carefully, exhaled carefully. Blinked her eyes carefully. She could understand the concept of cellular memory without deciding whether or not she believed any of it.

She realized what Wade was going to tell her, but there was a loud buzzing in her ears. She stared at him, saw his lips move, but heard nothing except the buzzing. First it buzzed low, then it buzzed high. Buzz, buzz, buzz. Buzzzzzzzz.

"Dixie? Dixie!" He reached across the coffee table separating them and squeezed her knee, giving it a little shake. "Dixie?"

Dixie shook herself out of the ridiculous trance or whatever she'd been in. "I'm sorry," she said, her mind clear now, clear and vehemently denying the silly idea that kept leaping at her. An idea that was preposterous.

"Dixie?"

She pushed herself to her feet. "That's an incredible story," she said. "I'm sorry you had to go through such a traumatic experience. I assume that everything went well. You look perfectly healthy to me."

"I am healthy, especially if I keep up with my meds and exercise."

"Oh, well, that's wonderful." She started toward the front door, her movements sharp and jerky. "I'm really glad for you."

"Dixie, come sit down."

"You've said what you came to say. Oh." She stopped and turned around. "I forgot your check. Wait here."

"Dixie, sit down."

Her eyes were overbright. Her hands fluttered in the air. "I'm glad you came by to tell me this, but I don't have time right now to—"

"Dixie." He stood and grabbed her wrist. "Stop it. You need to let me finish."

"No." She shook her head hard and tried to back away. "No, you're finished."

"I'm not."

"You have to be," she said frantically.

He saw the refusal in her eyes. Refusal to believe, to hear. "Dixie, I have to tell you."

"Why?" she cried, her voice and expression desperate.

"Because it's why I'm here. You already know the truth, don't you?"

"No." She shook her head. "Of course not." She shook her head again. "How could I?"

"Come," he said gently, pulling on her arm. "Sit with me."

She was breathing as if she'd just run a mile or more.

"Right here." He finally got her to sit next to him on the sofa. He turned until his knees pressed against hers, and they faced each other. He took her hands in his. Hers were trembling. His wanted to.

"Dixie, I got Jimmy Don's heart."

"Oh, God." She pulled her hands free and jumped up. "Oh, God. Oh, God." She stood there before the sofa and stared at him. "Oh, my God."

Wade hadn't known what to expect from her, but he'd known there would be a reaction. And here it was. He just didn't know what it meant. "Is it that bad a thing?" he asked. "That I got his heart?"

"Bad?" Dixie frowned, pressing her fingertips to her forehead. The buzzing was trying to drown out Wade's voice and even her own thoughts. "No," she said slowly. "It's just…I never expected… Wow." Her legs went out from under her and she sat abruptly on the coffee table. All efforts at denying what she'd known to be true from the instant he'd said "hug my two best boys" faded and left her limp.

Oh, good God, she thought. She was falling in love with Jimmy Don's heart? Been there, done that.

No, no, no. That wasn't right. It was Wade she was falling for.

A wash of fresh energy flooded her. "Why didn't you tell me?" she demanded. "Why did you let me have these feelings for you before you told me?"

He leaned toward her. "You have feelings for me?"

Dixie realized she'd said too much. "Never mind that. What are we going to tell the boys? And Pops? No. We can't tell them. They'll freak out."

"Like you did?"

She frowned. "They won't understand."

"They don't talk about their dad."

"They barely remember him. It's been two years."

"When anyone mentions their dad, what do they say?"

"Who, the boys, or…?"

"Either. Both."

Dixie shrugged. "I don't know. That he was good with horses, usually. Or somebody tells a story about his antics in high school."

"Does anybody tell them how special he was?"

She blinked. "Special? No."

"I want to, Dixie. I want his sons to know that he was a very special man." Wade took a deep, shuddering breath. "A hero, to me and several other people whose lives he saved or made bearable. I owe him that, and more."

Inside her chest, Dixie felt a tightening ease. "Oh, Wade, no. If Jimmy Don could tell you himself he'd say you don't owe him anything. He wasn't like that. He didn't do things because he expected something in return. He just did what he wanted to do. Sometimes it was a good deed, sometimes it was a good job. Sometimes, most of the time, he was just plain irresponsible. In a funny, lovable way, of course."

"Let me ask you this. When you get your driver's license renewed, do you check the organ donor box on it?"

She smiled slightly. "No."

"Why not?"

"Because I'm always afraid I'll get injured and the ambulance driver's mother will have been waiting for years for a new liver or something, and they'll see I'm a donor and take mine. Poof. I'm a goner, when I didn't have to be. I know it's silly, but—"

"It's very common. Let's face it. It takes courage to check that box on the license. Jimmy Don had that courage, Dixie. In my book he's a hero, and I want his sons to know that."

Dixie rubbed her hands up and down her arms. "This is going to upset them, and I hate to do that. They'll get sad. It will be like they've lost him all over again."

They reached for each other and grasped hands, holding tightly to each other, their gazes locked, his pleading for understanding, hers clouded with shock and confusion.

"Will you think about it?" Wade asked. "If you didn't want to tell them yourself, I could do it. And there's Pops to consider. Don't you think he'd want to know?"

"Yes." She swallowed hard. "Yes, Pops should know. But I have to think about the boys."

They sat there a moment, in the quiet of the house. Outside, a car engine revved in the next-door neighbor's driveway, and another car drove down the street way too fast for an area where children played. Someone nearby yelled at them to slow down.

"So, what do you think?" Wade asked. "Not about the boys, just…the whole thing."

She gave a half laugh. "I don't know. I mean, it's a miracle. Jimmy Don did something good by being an organ donor, then he did something stupid by getting himself killed, and because of those two things, you're alive and here and…it's all so…incredible."

"Do you think…we can still be friends? You and I?"

Dixie gave him a small smile. "No more big surprises?"

"Cross my heart." He did just that, crossed his heart with a forefinger.

A soft look came over Dixie's face. Slowly she reached out and placed one hand flat over his heart and stared, not at his face but at that hand covering his heart.

The warmth of her touch seeped clear through to his bones. "That's a miracle you're feeling."

She swallowed and looked up at him. "It feels strong."

"It is. And I thank God for it with every breath I take."

When she took her hand away, she took her

warmth with her. Neither spoke for a long time while she sat and simply stared at his chest.

Finally he felt the need to speak. "Am I still fired?"

Dixie smiled tiredly. "I can't imagine why you'd want to come back to work, now that your secret is out."

"You're shorthanded, remember? And as for my identity, if you don't mind, I'd rather not broadcast it."

"Somebody already has." She gestured toward the television.

Wade shrugged. "If people know, they know. We just don't have to inform them. I won't be able to stay too much longer, because someone is going to spot me and call the tabloids. If they show up I'll have to leave. They'd think nothing of tearing this town apart to get whatever photos they wanted."

"You're saying they're as bad in person as they seem on TV?"

"When it's you they're after, they're worse."

"But you're coming to work tomorrow?"

"I'll be there," he said. "If you like Miguel, you should keep him. Obviously, I don't need the money."

She gave him a half smile. "You mean after Pops comes back, I really can fire you?"

"Are you trying to ruin my résumé? When Pops comes back, I'll resign. I'm giving you notice, and my replacement has already been hired. I trained him myself."

"Well, then." She didn't know what else to say.

Didn't know what to do, how to act. Jimmy Don's heart beat in Wade's chest. It was too much to take in.

"Dixie?"

"Yes?"

"I might have his heart, and I might have come here because of his sons, but I'm not him. Do you understand what I'm saying?"

"I never thought you were him," she claimed.

"Just so you don't start looking for any more of his traits in me. I came here for the boys. Just to make sure they were all right since losing their father. I stayed because, yes, they were all right, because their mother made sure of it. I've stayed because of you, Dixie."

Dixie's vision blurred. "What are you saying?"

"I'm saying that the only thing I have now of Jimmy Don's is a physical organ. The feelings I have for you, for the boys, are mine, not his. They have nothing to do with cellular memory or transplanted organs."

She swallowed again. "How do you know? How can you be sure?"

"It's easy," he said with a shrug. "I just ask myself, if I'd met you before I got sick, would I feel the same way. The answer is…absolutely."

Dixie let out a breath she hadn't been aware of holding. "Maybe you'd better tell me what you mean when you say you have feelings for me."

"I mean, I care about you, Dixie," he said earnestly. "I care very much. It may go deeper than that, I don't know."

She snorted. "So what you're saying is you want to sleep with me."

His smile was fast and a tad wolfish. "Of course I do. I'm not dead, am I? But that's not what this is all about."

"It's not, huh? A man who could have any woman he wants just by crooking his finger in her direction, and he hangs around washing dishes in Tribute, Texas. I have to figure he expects to get something out of it."

"Look, I know I took you by surprise with all of this."

"That's the understatement of the century."

"All I planned to throw at you tonight was my background and my transplant. You're the one who brought up feelings and sex."

"Well, pardon the hell out of me."

"No pardon needed," he told her. There was a devil getting loose inside of him, one who wanted to see how far he could push her. On the other hand, a good, healthy argument about sex was bound to take her mind off her other concerns. Or not. But he didn't seem to have any option but to go for it. "It's fine with me if you want to talk about having sex. Personally, the way I feel, and guessing at the way you feel, I'd say we'll probably be making love rather than simply scratching an itch."

Her bright blue eyes widened. "We'll— You talk like it's a foregone conclusion that we're going to end up in bed together."

Wade shook off that devil and regained his sanity. Sort of. "I'm sorry. I didn't mean to be presumptuous. Call it wishful thinking on my part."

She took a slow, deep breath. "I do not believe we're talking about this. Arguing about it."

"About sex?"

The sound that came from her throat sounded suspiciously like a growl. "All of it," she claimed, waving her arms in the air. "You're stinking rich and washing my dishes with Jimmy Don's heart beating away in your chest, for crying out loud. I've known Jimmy Don since first grade, and loved him all my life, but even I know he was an irresponsible kid who never wanted to grow up. Lovable, yes, but irresponsible.

"You think he wanted you to check on his sons? Oh, he loved them, all right. In fact, he called me the night he died, and the last thing he said was for me to hug his two best boys for him. You got the words right, you know. He always said it just that way, his two best boys.

"But I'll lay you dollars to doughnuts that when he shut off his phone and stepped out in front of that taxicab and got himself killed, he was much more likely to be thinking about where to get his next beer. And now you come here and tell me he's a hero because he saved your life. Well, good for him. He finally did something right. And...oh, God, I didn't mean that."

She covered her mouth with both hands and squeezed her eyes shut. "I can't believe I said that."

She was both appalled and ashamed of herself for even thinking such a thing. It was accurate; Jimmy Don thought a great deal more about beer than most other things, but he'd loved his sons, he'd loved Pops and he'd loved her. He was merely a little boy who never grew up.

She was as much to blame for that as he was, she knew. She had always taken charge and made the decisions. When he let something slide, she jumped in and took care of it. Even in school, she'd done her best to keep him from getting in trouble. He'd just been so damned adorable, she hadn't been able to help herself. And it was hard to ever be angry with a guy who looked at you as if you'd hung the moon.

"Forget about it," Wade told her.

"No." She shook her head vehemently. "I don't want you thinking of him that way. It's not fair. Jimmy Don was a good man, honestly he was. He just wasn't a good husband after a while. But even after the divorce we were still best friends. We were better friends than we were spouses, actually."

Wade scratched his head. "Since that doesn't make sense to me, I'll take your word for it."

"Good." She nodded sharply. "And we'll forget about sex."

Wade widened his eyes and opened his mouth in an exaggerated look of shock. "Not on your life. You and I are destined to be together, so start getting used to the idea."

Dixie smirked. "Does that line work on the women in New York?"

He heaved a sigh. "Not so far."

She laughed.

He heaved another sigh, then turned serious. "Since we're obviously not going to be sleeping together tonight, do you want me to stay and help you tell the boys?"

She blinked a couple of times. She wasn't ready to be serious again. "Tell them that we're not sleeping together?"

"See, I knew you had sex on your mind," he claimed. "Deny it all you want, but it's there." He shook his head and *tsked* a couple of times. "I meant, tell them about how their dad saved my life."

"No." So, it was time to turn serious again, after all. "No, I want to think about that first. I'll tell Pops and talk it over with him."

"Do you want me to be there when you talk to him?"

She took a deep breath and let it out. "No, I think I should tell him on my own."

"You could send the boys back here to the house. I could stay with them while you talk to Pops at his place."

"I need to think about it all first. Let it all soak in."

"I guess I've hit you with a lot all at once."

"How about an avalanche?" she said wryly.

She stood, and so did he. She started to turn toward the door, but Wade stopped her with a hand on her arm.

"Dixie," he said softy. "I'm still me, you know."

"I'm still trying to figure out who that is."

"I'm sorry."

"For what?" she asked.

"For not telling you the truth sooner."

She searched his face for a long moment, then smiled softly. "Apology accepted."

Wade leaned toward her and brushed his lips across hers.

She kept her eyes open, looking directly into his deep brown eyes, and felt as if she were drowning. After a brief second of heated contact, she forced herself to step back. She needed to think, and for that she needed a clear mind. That didn't seem possible when she was around Wade.

"Okay," he said. "I'll go. But only if you promise that you don't hate me."

"I don't hate you, Wade," she said truthfully. "I promise. I just have a lot to think about."

"I know. I'll see you in the morning. Unless you want to talk later. If you do, just call me. Anytime, okay?"

"Okay."

She stood at her front door and watched one of the country's richest, most eligible bachelors walk away with Jimmy Don McCormick's heart. And maybe hers, too.

If that wasn't the damnedest thing.

Chapter Nine

When Dixie called the boys home, she asked Pops to come with them. When she got her sons into the tub, she took Pops to the kitchen, where the boys, who were not silent bathers by any means, would not overhear. There, once Pops was seated at the kitchen table with a dish of peach cobbler to work on, she told him first about Wade's true background and identity.

Unlike her, Pops didn't feel the least deceived. He laughed. "Ha! I knew there was more to that boy than he was lettin' on. Rich, you say?"

"Filthy rich."

"And him washing our dishes." He laughed again and shook his head. "Did he say why he was here?"

"Yes, he did." She told him the rest, about Wade's heart transplant, and where his new heart came from.

Pops cried. His tears were a mixture of renewed grief at the loss of his only grandson, and pride that a part of Jimmy Don lived on in another person. More than one person, most likely.

"That's something, isn't it?" He wiped the moisture from his cheeks and eyes. "I'm so proud of Jimmy Don, I think I might burst."

"I know what you mean, Pops." She stood next to him, leaned against him and wrapped her arms around him. "He did good, didn't he."

Sniff. "He sure did."

"Wade wants the boys to know."

Pops peered up at her. "You don't?"

Dixie sighed. "I don't know. I don't want them upset. They were devastated when their daddy died. Talking about this might bring all that back. They might get it in their heads that it's Wade's fault Jimmy Don died. That it's not fair for him to be dead and Wade to benefit from it."

"Is that what you think? That it's not fair for Wade to be alive while Jimmy Don's dead?"

"Me? No. Of course not."

Pops twisted away from her and looked at her more closely. "Well, something's got you all sideways."

"I don't know what you're talking about." She

pushed away and turned toward the sink to get a drink of water. And to keep him from seeing the sudden blush heating her cheeks.

"And if you believe that," he said, "I've got a six-legged dog I'll sell you."

"Pops, really. Why would I be upset about anything Wade says?"

"Maybe because him being so rich and all, he probably won't be working at the diner much longer. It's a cinch he doesn't need the job. Might not even hang around town for long. Unless, of course, a certain person was to give him a reason to stick around."

"Well, then," she said, jerking up his now empty cobbler dish and carrying it to the sink, "you better be thinking up a reason to give him if you want him to stay."

"Ha. Like you don't want him to stay."

"Why should I care one way or the other?"

"Dixie, you're gonna make an old man out of me before my time."

"That'll be the day. Besides, you lie about your age so much, nobody's quite sure how old you are. And I'm sure you prefer it that way. But if you really want to talk about someone's love life, you can tell me about your visit this afternoon from Ima Trotter."

"Hmph."

From where she stood, several feet away at the sink, Dixie noted that the tops of his ears turned red.

* * *

Wade wasn't sure what to expect the next morning when he met Dixie and the boys at the diner. The boys were their usual early-morning bickering selves. Dixie, however, would barely meet his eyes. He assumed that meant she was having trouble accepting and dealing with all he'd told her the night before. He couldn't say he blamed her. It had taken him considerable time to get used to the idea of having someone else's heart beating in his chest.

Come to that, he still wasn't used to the idea, but he sure liked the beating. He liked being alive. It was just that the means by which that was possible took getting used to. If Dixie needed more than one night to come to terms with it, he could give her time.

He just wished she would look at him.

Dixie wasn't ready to look at him. She wanted, badly, to have him put his arms around her and tell her everything was going to work out. And that was just stupid. When had she ever needed a man to tell her things were going to work out? She was used to handling things on her own, and had, to date, done a fairly decent job of it. She would continue to do so. To rely on someone else for happiness or stability or comfort or any other darn thing was to court disappointment, in her book.

To prove to herself that she didn't really want to be held, she took a big step back from Wade emotionally and, when possible, physically. Time enough later to deal with one of the country's richest, most eligible bachelors. All she wanted for today was for him to wait tables.

The day raced by in a blur of customers and orders and dirty dishes for Wade. He was getting pretty good at dealing with the customers and taking the orders.

Ima came in for lunch again.

"Good afternoon," Wade said, placing a menu and a glass of ice water before her.

"Oh, my, doesn't that look cool and refreshing. I declare, it's hot enough to fry eggs on the sidewalk out there."

"Is it? I haven't been outside since I came in this morning."

Actually, he thought, every time he got near Dixie it seemed a little on the cool side. He would have to do something about that soon. When Pops came back to work, the only way Wade was going to see Dixie during the day was if he came in and placed an order. No way could he go back to washing dishes and take Miguel's job away from him. The kid and his family appeared to have a serious need for money. Wade would not get in the way of the boy earning his pay, even if it was only minimum wage.

Ima took a long swallow of her ice water and set it down with a satisfied sigh. "Not very mannerly of me, guzzling my water that way, but it surely hit the spot. I think I'll stick with something on the cool side for lunch. Bring me a BLT and a small side salad with Italian dressing, if you please."

"Certainly." He liked this lady, with her snowy white hair and face full of lines that said she'd lived. "Iced tea?"

"Perfect," she said with a smile. "You tell that Dixie she'd better watch out. You're taking such good care of the customers, we may not want her back." There was a definite twinkle in her eyes.

Wade placed a hand on his hip and pulled out his best Southern accent. "Miz Ima, I've been telling her ιnat very thing since yesterday."

Ima cackled and swatted his arm. "Go on with you."

"Yes, ma'am. Be back with your sandwich and salad as soon as they're ready. Do you want to wait until then for your tea, or would you like it now?"

"You've learned your job quite well, young man. I'll take my tea with my meal, thank you."

Hers wasn't an order he needed to turn in. The bacon was already cooked, so he could build the sandwich himself, and fresh bowls of salad sat covered in plastic wrap in the cooler. Dixie had four other orders going on the grill and didn't need to be bothered. He built the sandwich, tore the cover off a salad and put both on a tray along with salad dressing and iced tea.

As he was serving Ima the meal a few moments later, the bell over the front door dinged, announcing yet another customer. Lunch business was booming. If this pace kept up, they could have a full house before long.

"Hey, Bill," someone called out.

Bill Gray, the newspaper editor, waved in response, then sat down at a table.

"Heard a rumor about you," the man at the next table said to Gray.

"Here you go, Miz Ima," Wade said, placing her lunch before her and listening with half an ear to the various conversations going on around the room. "Do you need anything else?"

"If it's about that last New Year's Eve party," Gray answered, "I did not dance on top of the table. That's my story, and I'm sticking to it."

"This looks just fine, Wade," Ima said. "Thank you."

"Naw, not that rumor. I know that one's not true."

"You should," Ima said, joining in the conversation as Wade turned away. "You started it, Jim."

"Miz Ima, you're not supposed to tell him that."

"It's all right, Miz Ima," Gray said. "I already knew who started it."

"Forget that. Old news, pardon the pun. This is a new rumor," Jim said. "I heard you were going to sell the paper and retire."

Wade paused on the other side of the counter and blatantly eavesdropped.

"Sell the paper?" Ima said, shocked. "Is this true, William?"

"Don't you think it's past time for a new voice in this town? It's time I retired, if I can find the right buyer," Gray said. "I promised my wife when we married that one day we'd live in paradise. As much as I love this town, paradise it's not. She's got her heart set on Hawaii."

Wade had to assume that Bill Gray had a good financial planner for him to be able to retire in Hawaii. There wasn't a great deal of profit, if any, in small-town weekly newspapers these days.

"What a fine man you are, William," Ima said, "to keep such a promise to your wife. Just do this town a favor and try not to sell the paper to some big conglomerate who'll manage it from New York, or someplace like that. We need a paper that's purely local."

"I've been worried about that very thing," Gray said.

"Order up!" Dixie called as she slapped the bell signaling an order was ready.

Wade filed the newspaper information away in his brain and pulled the burger from the order window.

And so the day went. Miguel kept up and seemed to be doing a good job. In the middle of the afternoon, with only a few customers on hand and none of them ready to check out, Wade saw Miguel come out to bus the two tables in the back, and used that opportunity to step into the kitchen to see Dixie.

"How are you holding up?" he asked.

Her smile looked tired, just as it had when she'd unlocked the door this morning.

"Pretty good," she answered. "How about you?"

"The same. Miz Ima says I'm so good you might be out of a job."

"Oh, really?" She flipped a ground beef patty on the grill. "What do you say?"

"I say you've got nothing to worry about. No way would I want to do this very often. I have enjoyed it, though."

"You have?"

"It's always educational to do someone else's job for a couple of days. Gives you a new perspective. Plus I enjoy meeting the people." He hesitated. "Were you able to decide about telling the boys?"

"That was slick. Start off talking about jobs, then, *wham,* hit me with what's really on your mind."

"Are you going to answer me?"

She sighed and met his gaze squarely for the first time that day. "Yes. It's your thing, so I want you to tell them. But I want to be there. And I want to talk to you before you tell them."

"That's fair. It's fine. Thank you, Dixie."

She shook her head. "I only hope it doesn't upset them."

"I think they might surprise you."

"Come have supper with us tonight," she said.

The heart in question did a little flip-flop. He hadn't expected an invitation to supper. "I'd love to. What time?"

"About six. We eat early."

"I'll be there. Oh, does Pops know?"

"About you and your heart? Yes."

Wade nodded. "Did he take it okay?"

She shrugged. "Better than I did. He agrees with you that Jimmy Don turned out to be a hero." She started to say more, but Miguel returned just then with a tubful of dirty dishes.

Wade got the message. She didn't want to talk in front of Miguel. He nodded toward the grill. "Is that burger about done?"

"Another minute or two. I'll holler."

"I'll get back out there, then."

She watched him walk out and wondered what other surprises he might throw at her before everything was said and done.

After work Wade showered and put on clean clothes, then killed a little time checking his e-mail. His mother was having a fit because he wasn't home yet. His sisters appeared to love the extra work piled on them since his illness. His father pretended to be irritated at having to go to the office nearly every day again, but Wade knew the man welcomed the chance to get away from the house, i.e. "Mother," as often as possible.

Wade knew his parents were not only deeply devoted to each other and in love, they were also crazy about each other. That did not mean, however, that Dad could hang around the house all day, as he'd done much of the time during the two years Wade had been running the corporation before his heart had decided to go on strike.

No, Mom kept a running list of projects that needed doing, and if someone was home, she considered them fair game. "If you're going to be underfoot, dear, why don't you take that box of clothes to the Goodwill," or, "There's a bag of canned goods on the kitchen counter that needs to go to the Food Pantry to help feel the homeless." Or, "The dog needs to go to the groomer today. You wouldn't mind taking him, would you? I thought not."

Telling Mother "No" took great fortitude and an ironclad reason. She could shoot holes in anything a hapless spouse or child could think of. After all, as she was fond of reminding them, nothing was more important than keeping Mother happy.

And, oddly enough, that was the exact truth. All of them loved the little tyrant so much, they would do anything for her. If she knew that—and she did— she never used it against you. Much.

With his e-mail taken care of for the time being, and the hour still a little early to show up at Dixie's, he decided to take a stroll down Main. There was something about Main Street in Tribute that appealed to him, especially around the town square. He liked the variety of shops and businesses, the friendliness of nearly everyone he passed on the sidewalk.

While he was out, maybe he would pick up some flowers for Dixie and a bottle of wine for dinner.

The five-o'clock rush hour in Tribute was naturally a far cry from the same event in Manhattan. Here traffic definitely picked up, but if there had ever been more than three cars per lane backed up at the town's only traffic light, it had probably been the homecoming parade for the high school.

As for walking, people generally scratched their heads and offered him a ride. If you couldn't park within twenty feet of the door to wherever you were going, the predominant course of action was to drive around the block a couple of times until a space opened up. And when you did park, it was usually an SUV or a pickup as opposed to an actual car.

As he approached the town square he eyed the gray granite courthouse on the south side, with its small, manicured park stretching out to form the center of the square, with a street on each of its other three sides. A wide sidewalk ran straight from the courthouse steps, all the way through the middle of the park to Main Street, opposite the courthouse.

A small sign at the curb proclaimed the green lawn as City Park. In the middle of the east side of the park stood a large monolith of dark granite. Wade had studied it up close. He'd stood back and watched as others approached it. Some walked away in tears, others with a sigh. On it were engraved the names of all the town's war dead. The first listing was a man killed in 1889 in the Spanish-American War. The most recent, a woman in the Army National Guard killed in Iraq earlier this year.

There was a separate, smaller monument listing those who'd died in what the monument called the War Between the States. It was divided down the middle, one side for those who'd fought for the North, the other for Southerners.

Wade stood near the Civil War monument and glanced across the street toward the newspaper office. So Gray was going to sell out and retire? How interesting.

Glancing at his watch, he realized he'd killed a little more time than he'd meant to. He picked up his pace and bought a small bouquet of mixed flowers at the grocery store down the block. He decided against the wine. He would save that for a time when it would be only Dixie and himself. And that time would definitely come, he vowed. She was much too important to him; he couldn't keep away from her for any length of time. Even if she wouldn't go out with him, he would simply keep asking. She couldn't say no forever, right?

But first he had to get through tonight, with the boys. He prayed to find the right words with which to tell them what their father meant to him.

* * *

It was disconcerting, Wade admitted silently, to find himself more nervous as he approached the McCormick house than he was that day a couple of weeks ago when he stood before Dixie's Diner for the first time and wondered what he might find inside.

He'd found a whole new world. A minimum-wage job as dishwasher, he remembered with a smile. But before that he'd found a woman who captured his mind and, it seemed, his heart. He'd found a friend in Pops. He'd found two young boys who very soon had come to mean the world to him. He'd found a community that fascinated him, called to something inside him, made him feel welcome and at home.

Now if he didn't find the right words for what he had to say, he could hurt Ben and Tate, and that was absolutely the last thing on earth he wanted to do. So, please God, let the right words be there for him.

He started up Dixie's street, and there they were, those two bright, happy, fun boys of hers, running toward him as if he was their best friend in the world and they hadn't seen him in years.

It had been two hours.

"Wade! Wade!"

"Mom says you're coming for supper."

"Flowers? What're those for?" Ben asked.

Tate jabbed his older brother in the ribs with his elbow. "That's what guys do, they bring flowers to the lady when they have supper."

"What do *you* know." Ben shoved Tate away.

"Do you know what etiquette is?" Wade asked.

Dancing around and beside him as he walked up the street, the boys snorted and giggled.

"That's like, Don't talk with your mouth full," Ben said.

"Yeah, and saying *please* and *thank you*," Tate added.

"That's right," Wade said. "It also means that when a lady invites you to dinner in her home, you should take her a hostess gift. I decided on flowers. You think she'll like them?" He held them out for inspection.

Both boys shrugged. "Sure," Tate said.

"Prob'ly," Ben decided. "Girls like junk like flowers."

Junk. Wade smiled.

Ben and Tate marched him up the steps and through the front door.

"Mom!" Ben yelled.

"Wade's here!" Tate hollered.

Wade pursed his lips as Dixie stuck her head around the corner from the kitchen. "You don't have to yell. I'm right here. Hi, Wade. Glad you could make it."

"He brought flowers." Ben didn't sound any too impressed with the idea.

"Thank you," Dixie told Wade. "They're beautiful. Let me put them in water. Boys, go tell Pops it's time to eat. Help him get over here if he needs it. Then wash up. Supper's ready."

"Yes, ma'am," they said in unison.

As they raced past her for the back door, she shook her head. "I won't throw your food out if you walk," she called.

They didn't slow down until they hit the door of Pops's apartment.

Wade studied Dixie as she stared out the window into her backyard. He didn't know how to ask what he wanted to know, so he asked something else. "Are you going to be okay with Miguel?"

She glanced at him a moment, then took a vase from a cabinet and filled it with water. "You're really not coming back?" She took her time arranging the flowers in the vase.

"I can't justify taking a job somebody else needs, when I don't need the money."

"Oh. Yeah. Right. Stupid question. I forgot you're rich. Here come Pops and the boys." She moved to the stove and took the lid off a pan of spaghetti sauce.

The spicy aroma made Wade's mouth water. "Smells great."

"It's Pops's recipe. When the chamber of commerce meets for lunch once a month in the banquet room, this is what they order."

"Heck of a recommendation—the entire chamber of commerce. By the way," he added, hearing the boys and Pops near the back door. "If Pops needs to stay home for another day or two, I can wait tables again. I'm getting pretty good at it."

"Maybe if we put a sign out front—'come in and be served by one of the country's richest, most eligible bachelors'—we'd fill the place up." Her tone was snappish and biting.

"I'm not going to apologize for being rich, Dixie. Some of it I inherited, some of it I earned. Either way, I find it a source of pride, not shame. I'm sorry it upsets you."

Her shoulders slumped. "No, I'm sorry. It's silly of me. I just had this nice little fantasy going on in my head—"

He grinned. "You've been fantasizing about me?"

"—and now I find out you're a different person."

"I'm not. I'm the same man I was last week, Dixie. My money and my new heart don't change who I am inside. What's changed is your perception of me."

Dixie knew she was procrastinating when she made the boys wipe down the counters and the table a second time. The dishes were in the dishwasher, ready to be washed. She didn't run the machine until bedtime, because it was hard to hear the television over the noise. Everything else was neater than usual.

"C'mon, Mom, are we through?"

"All right," she said with a sigh. "Let's go to the living room."

"Awright!" The boys slapped hands, then bumped butts. Then raced the entire five feet to the living room.

With another sigh, Dixie followed at a much more sedate pace. She pulled the boys with her to the sofa and sat down between them so the three of them faced Wade in the easy chair and Pops in the recliner. "Wade has something he wants to talk to you guys about. Pops, are you sticking around for this?"

"Thought I would, if Wade doesn't mind."

"Mind? I'd be relieved."

Pops nodded in acknowledgment.

"What do you wanna talk to us about, Wade? Little League?"

"No, silly." Ben reached around Dixie and gave Tate a disdainful shove. "He's going to tell us he's leaving."

"What makes you say a thing like that?" Dixie demanded, stunned.

Ben shrugged and studied the toe of his sneaker. "What else you gonna do when Pops goes back, fire Miguel? I'm not dumb, you know."

"No." Dixie wrapped her arm around him and kissed the top of his head. "No, you're not dumb." She pulled Tate to her with the other arm and kissed him, too. "Neither are you. You're both pretty darn smart. Now let's be quiet and listen to what Wade has to say."

They looked over at Wade expectantly.

Wade wiped his damp palms along the thighs of his jeans. "First, I'm not leaving town. At least, not right away. But you're right about Miguel. If he works out, he needs the job a lot worse than I do. You see, I don't need the money at all. I've got enough money without having to work."

"Are you rich?" Tate asked.

"Yes. I'm what most people consider rich."

"Is that what you wanted to tell us?" Ben asked.

"No, not really. But I did want you to know that. Not because I like to brag about being rich, but because you might hear it from somebody else in town, and I'd rather you hear it from me first. Are you okay with it?"

"Sure."

"Thank you," Wade told them. "There's something important I need to explain to you, but I'm not sure exactly how to make you understand, because it's pretty complicated."

Wade thought for a moment, then looked at the boys. "Have you two ever had a dog?"

"Yeah. His name was Tippy," Ben said.

"He got hit by a car and died," Tate added.

"I'm sorry. That's tough. You must have been pretty sad."

"We had a funeral and everything."

"I'll bet Tippy appreciated that."

The boys shrugged and looked down at their feet.

It was all Wade could do to keep his hands and voice steady. He didn't want to screw this up. He had to make them understand, and he wanted, desperately, for them to accept him as readily after he explained as they had before.

"How would you have felt," he said, "if, when Tippy got hit by that car, there was another dog, on the other side of town, who was very sick. His heart was failing him, even though he wasn't very old. He was so sick that the vet said that if he didn't get a new heart, the poor pup wouldn't last the night. And what if they could do dogs like they do people—they could do organ transplants. What would you think if they wanted to take Tippy's heart, because Tippy's not using it anymore, and put it in this sick dog across town? Would that be okay with you?"

Tate shrugged and grimaced. "I dunno. I guess."

Ben looked thoughtful. "Would we get to watch?"

Leave it to boys, Wade thought wryly. "I don't know. I don't think they let spectators in the operating rooms. You know, because of germs."

"Yeah, I guess you're right," Ben said.

Tate still seemed to be having trouble with the idea.

"What if I told you that Tippy had signed a donor card before he died, saying he wanted his organs to go to other dogs when he died."

"Dogs?" Ben asked. "More than one?"

"Well, a dog's got lots of organs, just like a person. There's a heart, lungs, two kidneys, a liver."

Tate perked up. "Eyeballs?"

"Why not?" Wade said.

"What about the tongue? Would they want Tippy's tongue?"

Wade smiled at Tate's sudden enthusiasm. "I don't

know. It would depend on whether or not another dog needed a new one, I guess. Would all that be all right with you guys?"

"Sure," Tate said.

"It's the same as organ donation in people, right?"

"You know about that?" Wade asked. "About people donating their organs when they die?"

"Sure," Ben said.

Dixie ran her fingers through Ben's hair. "Where did you learn about organ transplants, honey?"

"I dunno." Ben shrugged and flopped his hands out. "School. We talked about it a lot last year when the teacher's daddy had a kidney transplant up in Dallas."

"How about you?" Dixie asked Tate. "Did you talk about this at school, too?"

"Sure," he said with a shrug. "But that was about people. We didn't talk about dogs."

"Okay, wise guy," Dixie said to Wade with a smile. "Now you have to turn it around."

"I've got it," he told her. "Would it surprise you boys to know that your dad was an organ donor?"

"Our dad?" Ben asked.

"Really?" Tate asked.

"Really," Wade answered.

Ben turned his head slightly and peered at Wade out of one eye for a long moment. He crossed his arms and leaned back, still eyeing Wade thoughtfully. "How come you know about our dad?"

"Because when your dad died, I was like that sick

dog across town. My heart was quitting. I'd been in the hospital in New York City for weeks. They told me I had to have a new heart or I was going to die. It got really bad. A couple of hearts became available, but they didn't match with me, so they went to someone else who needed a heart. Lots and lots of people need new organs, and not very many people donate their organs."

"You got our dad's heart?" Ben asked.

"I did, Ben. I was dying. They told me if I lived through the night it would be a miracle. My mom and dad and sisters were all there in my hospital room, praying for a miracle. And then a terrible thing happened. Your dad got hit by that cab in New York, and he died. I know that made all of you very sad, because you loved him very much, and he loved you."

"I cried," Ben said, hanging his head.

"We all did, honey." Dixie hugged him to her side. "We all cried, for days and days, because we missed him and didn't want him to die."

Tate sniffed. "So they, like, put his heart in you and made it start beating again?"

"That's exactly what they did, Tate. It saved my life. And I want you to know, I want all of you to know, how grateful I am that he was brave enough to sign that donor card and have it marked on his driver's license. He was a brave, brave man, your dad was. A generous man, and I know he loved the two of you more than anything in the world."

"Did it hurt?" Ben asked.

"Did what hurt?" Dixie asked.

"The what-do-you-call-it, the transplant. Did it hurt?"

"I was pretty sore for several days after the surgery, but they knocked me out for the operation, so I never knew."

"Jerry Beaver had his appendix out and he's got a cool scar. Do you have a scar?" Tate asked.

Wade smiled slightly. "I do, and it's a doozie. Runs from my neck to my navel."

Both boys' eyes widened with awe.

"Wow," Tate said with what sounded a great deal like reverence. "Can we see?"

"Tate, what a question," Dixie protested.

Wade winked at Tate. "Girls get squeamish about that sort of thing. Maybe I'll show you sometime when there are no girls around."

"So," Pops said easily, "you've got Jimmy Don's heart beating right there in your chest."

"That's right," Wade said. "How do you feel about that, Pops?"

"I think it's a miracle that part of my grandson is alive and beating long after he's gone. I'm proud that he was able to save your life that way."

Wade felt a lump the size of a golf ball rise in his throat. "Thanks, Pops. That means a lot to me." He looked over at the boys, one on each side of their mother. He looked at their mother. "It would mean even more if the rest of you felt that way, because I've got to tell you, as far as I'm concerned, boys, your dad is the biggest hero I've ever known."

Their eyes got big and round.

Tate swallowed and looked up at his mom. "A hero? Our dad's a hero?"

"Well," she said, putting her arm around him, "he saved Wade's life, and probably several other lives, too. I guess that makes him the best kind of hero, don't you think?"

"Golly." Ben couldn't seem to take his eyes off Wade. Then he blinked and looked up at Dixie. "Does that mean his name will go on the monument at city hall?"

Wade's heart gave a little thump inside his chest.

"Naw, son," Pops said. "That's for people who got killed in wars."

Ben frowned. "That doesn't seem right. A hero's a hero, isn't he? How come some of 'em get a monument and some don't?"

"I don't know," Pops said. "That's just the way it is."

"Don't you worry," Wade told Ben. "We'll figure out some way to make sure everyone knows what a hero your dad was. That's why I came to town in the first place. To make sure my heart donor's sons were all right, and to make sure his hometown knew what a good man he was."

"Golly," Ben said again.

"Well," Dixie said to the room in general. "Wade's given us all a lot to think about, hasn't he. But right now it's bath time for you two. Say good night to Wade."

The boys wanted to argue, but Dixie was having none of it. She stood firm and in a few moments had them headed for the bathroom.

"Good night, Wade," they said together.

Ben paused behind his brother. "Wade? I'm glad you didn't die. I'm glad our dad's heart saved you."

Wade's vision blurred. "Me, too, Ben. Thanks."

"Come on, boys," Dixie ordered from the doorway to the hall. "Let's go."

Wade slumped back in his chair and watched them disappear down the hall. A minute later he heard bathwater running.

He was so relieved to have that discussion behind him, he felt weak with it.

"You handled that real good," Pops said.

"Thanks. I've faced angry shareholders, irate employees and mutinous boards of directors, and none of them were as scary as this was."

Pops chuckled. "Yep, kids can be tough. But these two do all right."

"They're the most well-adjusted kids I've ever seen. You and Dixie, and I guess their dad before he died, have definitely been doing something right."

"It's Dixie more than me, and damn sure more than

Jimmy Don. He was my grandson and I loved him to pieces, but about the only things he taught those boys was how to ride a horse and how to lie around on the couch and watch TV. And he went and sold their horse to pay his entry fee in a rodeo up in Kansas. Broke their little hearts, he did. But he loved them. And he loved that girl in there, too. He just didn't know how to be a husband or a daddy. Hell, I don't think he ever figured out how to be a grown-up. But I guess you don't need to hear about all his flaws."

"Not really." Wade smiled. "He did all right by me. That's all I care about."

"You gonna leave town, now that you've come clean about who you are?"

Wade leaned forward and braced his elbows on his knees. "I don't know."

"You want some advice from an old codger who never learned how to mind his own business?"

"I don't know about that, but I'd take advice from you any day of the week."

Pops chuckled. "I'd say if a man had leanings toward a certain woman, he ought to ask himself, is there anything better than this waiting back home for me? Forget the job, forget all them damn directors and employees. None of them can keep a man warm at night or sit beside him when he's old. This is a good town. Or, if it came down to it, probably wouldn't hurt a certain woman and her boys to see a bit of the world, maybe move to New York."

Wade closed his eyes briefly. "Are you giving me your blessing, Pops?"

"I would never do such a thing. I'm just saying, is all."

"Thank you, Pops. Thank you. But I'm not sure the woman in question wants what you and I might want. She was none too happy to find out who I really am. It could be that she's hoping to see the last of me."

"Well now, that's your job, boy. You're supposed to convince her she can't live without you."

Chapter Ten

"Mom?"

Dixie stopped in the bedroom doorway in the act of turning off the light. She'd just put her boys to bed and kissed them good-night, twice. "What is it, Ben?"

"Do you mind that they cut Dad up and took out his heart to save Wade?"

"No," she said softly. "I don't mind at all, honey, because I know it's what your dad wanted. He wanted his organs to go to people who needed them after he was through with them."

"I guess that ol' taxicab saw to it that he was through with them, huh?" piped up Tate.

The resilience of children never ceased to amaze her. She was still shaky on the inside, and they were so matter-of-fact about it all. "It sure did, Tater. Now, you two need to get to sleep."

"G'night, Mom."

"'Night, Mom."

"'Night-'night, sweethearts. I love you."

Dixie turned off the light, stepped out of the room and pulled the door closed. She leaned her back against it and closed her eyes, saying a quick but heartfelt prayer of gratitude that the boys seemed to have understood about the transplant and accepted it without a qualm.

Pops had not only accepted it, he'd celebrated the news. All she had to do now was find her own way through the tangle of feelings inside herself to know how she felt about it.

But really, she asked herself, what was there to consider? Was she going to think less of Wade because he'd had a heart transplant? Or because the heart happened to be Jimmy Don's? Thinking less of him for either reason—and neither was his fault— would be incredibly small and mean-spirited of her, and she had never been particularly small or mean-spirited, if she said so herself.

What, then, was left to consider? What had made her hide in her bedroom rather than return to the living room and their guest while the boys took their bath? What was it that nagged at the back of her mind?

Ah, yes. Cha-ching. The money. His wealth was harder to accept than Jimmy Don's heart beating in his chest, because in the end it would be that wealth that took him away from her. He'd only come to see about the boys. He'd told her that. He said he'd stayed because of her, but that, she assumed, was more flattery than fact. He'd stayed until he could decide how to tell them who he was.

Now he'd told them. He had no more reason to stay. Now, she feared, he would leave. Maybe not tomorrow, maybe not the next day but soon. Very soon. All that money would pull him back to New York, to the luxuries, the life he was used to.

How had she let herself fall for a man who would not stay?

She didn't know what to say to him, how to face him with this new self-knowledge. Yet, curling up in a ball on her bed was not a viable option. She'd never been a coward, never feared her own feelings before. She didn't intend to start now.

With that little pep talk under her belt, she pushed away from her sons' bedroom door, squared her shoulders and headed for the living room.

She rounded the corner and stopped short. "Where's Wade?"

Pops stretched back in his recliner and shifted his weight. "Went home. Said to tell you good-night."

"Oh."

Pops eyed her carefully, correctly interpreting

the disappointment hunching her shoulders. "Is that something you're going to get used to? Him being gone?"

"I might as well." She ran her fingers through her hair. "He's done what he came to town to do. He won't stick around long now."

"Maybe," he said oh, so casually, "all he needs is a reason to stay. Maybe," he added, "he needs a little encouragement."

"And maybe," she said direly, "he can't wait to shake the dust of this two-bit town off his Ferragamos."

"His what?"

"Fancy shoes."

"Only shoes I've seen him wear since he hit town are sneakers."

"It was just an expression."

"A telling one," he said.

"What are you talking about?"

"You. By golly, I think you're a snob," he declared.

Dixie was shocked. "Pops! Why would you say such a thing? I'm not a snob. I'm not in a position to turn my nose up at anybody."

"But you just did. What do they call it? Reverse snobbery, that's it."

"Why, because I made a crack about Wade's shoes? It was just an expression. I didn't mean anything by it, for heaven's sake."

"Hmph. I think you don't like him anymore, now that you found out he's rich."

"Don't be silly, Pops. I'm just trying to be realistic. He didn't come here to get involved with me or anyone else. He came to see about the boys, and he's done that. Why are we having this conversation?"

"Beats the hell outta me. You could be right, anyway."

"I'm what?" She cupped a hand to her ear. "I don't think I heard that. What did you say?"

Pops chuckled. "Yeah, yeah, I said you were right. Maybe."

"Eureka! About what?"

"About Wade maybe leaving."

Dixie threw her hands in the air. "I give up. Now you're arguing my side?"

He shrugged. "It's just that you didn't give him a by-your-leave when you left with the boys. I think you hurt his feelings. Made him feel unwanted."

"Oh, come on. It was bath time. He's got thicker skin than that," she protested.

"Yeah, you're probably right," he said, doubt in his voice.

"Oh, for heaven's sake." Dixie jumped up from the sofa and headed for the door. "I'm going out for a breath of air. Will you stay in the house until I get back?"

Pops smirked. "Only if you promise to stay gone all night."

"Pops! I'm shocked. Truly shocked." And more

embarrassed than she remembered being in ages, she thought as she slammed out of the house.

The air was warm and humid, the sky dark. Here on her street, with the streetlight so near, only a few stars were visible.

She decided to walk. Not that she was going anyplace in particular. She just wanted to get out for a bit. Still, wherever she ended up would be nobody's business. Having her car parked somewhere would only create questions, cause talk. No. Walking was the thing.

As long as no one saw her, she thought. They'd stop and ask if she was all right. Nobody walked in Tribute.

She took the residential streets.

Wade didn't go straight home. He was too wound up. He needed to burn off some of the tension coiling in his gut. He walked to the high school and the track behind it. This time of night, the student athletes were finished with it for the day.

The track enclosed the high school football field. It sat in a flat bowl, with small hills surrounding it. The houses on those hills had backyards that looked down on the field. The cheap seats for football games. Cheap if you didn't count the mortgage.

He stepped onto the track and started walking faster until, by the first turn, he was jogging. By the back stretch, he was running all-out. The dark didn't bother him. There was enough light from the houses above to guide him. And he'd been running here several times during the past couple of weeks. He felt as if he could run it with his eyes closed, but he decided not to try it.

He ran until all he thought about was the pounding of his feet, the burning of his calves. The beating of his heart.

He did four laps, then slowed down and walked a fifth. Jeans and dress shirt, even short-sleeved, were not good running attire. He wasn't normally sweating this much after four laps. And he wasn't likely to cool down much, either, in this humidity. He looked forward to hitting the shower.

But when he turned up his sidewalk and finally looked up at his door, he forgot about the shower. He stopped cold and stared. His heart started racing as if he were back on the track. "Dixie? What are you doing here?"

Dixie rose from his stoop and brushed off the seat of her jeans. What was she doing here? She had no clue. Probably making a fool out of herself. But, as the saying went, no guts, no glory.

"I came to talk to you."

He glanced around, up and down the street. "Where's your car?"

"Worried about your reputation if I stay too late?"

"What?"

"Never mind. I took a page from your book and

walked. You must have taken the long way, since I beat you."

"I went to the track and ran."

"Oh, well, it was none of my business, anyway. I shouldn't have just dropped in on you this way. Shouldn't have presumed—"

"Dixie." His voice was softer than the air around her. His fingers touching her cheek sent a shiver of heat racing down her spine. "You can presume anything you want about me. Or you can just ask. Or drop by and sit on my stoop whenever you want."

She couldn't think, couldn't breathe. She stepped back far enough that his hand dropped away from her face. All she could think to say was, "Okay."

"Come on in." He pushed the door open and motioned her inside. "It's not much, but it's home."

She knew she should turn around and go home, but she found herself stepping through the door and into his apartment. *"Not much"* was an understatement. From what she could see, there were only two rooms, and they were small. There was a water stain on the ceiling. The furniture must have come with the place; she couldn't imagine Wade purchasing the worn, outdated sofa and chair on purpose.

"You live here?"

"I do. Can I get you something to drink? I've got soft drinks, orange juice and water."

"Wade, you *live* here? You live *here?*"

"Yes, Dixie, I live here."

She turned in a slow circle. The walls seemed freshly painted, but that was the best she could say for the place. It was small and dark and depressing. *"Why?"*

"Because I got tired of staying at the motel. I needed a place to live. This was available. What's your problem?"

He was sounding testy, and she couldn't blame him. She was insulting his home, as it were. She just couldn't help it. "With all your money, why are you living in this dump?"

"Ah, that's it. I'm rich, so this is beneath me."

She grimaced. "When you put it like that it sounds stupid." Had Pops been right? *Was* she a snob? "I'm sorry," she said. "You're right. If I'd come here last week, I wouldn't have thought a thing about it. Now I've offended you and that's the last thing I wanted to do."

With a hand to her lower back, he took her farther into the room so he could close the door. That touch felt…intimate. Too intimate. It made her want to turn into him and wrap herself in his arms.

"If that was the last thing you wanted, what was the first?"

Dixie turned to face him. She had to get her brain working again. "I'm sorry. What?"

He peered at her closely. "Are you feeling all right?"

"Of course. Why wouldn't I?" Oh, and wasn't that a stupid question. She was acting like a zombie. With attention deficit disorder.

"Because you don't seem like yourself. What I said tonight is no more than we talked about last night. Was there something there that bothered you? And you never did say if you wanted anything to drink."

"I'll have a soda. And no, nothing bothered me any more tonight than it did last night. I want to thank you for how you handled things with the boys, thank you for what you gave them of their father."

"Dixie." He trailed his fingers across her cheek, as he'd done outside on the stoop.

Her knees turned to jelly.

"You don't have anything to thank me for."

He lowered his hand and moved the eight feet or so from the front door to the refrigerator in his kitchen and took out two cans. "Do you want it in a glass with ice?"

"No. Thanks. The can is fine."

"Okay, then." He handed her the can, then took her other hand in his. "Come sit down and talk to me." He led her to the sofa, then sat in the chair across from her.

When he released her, the heat from his touch stayed in her hand. She was grateful she wasn't trembling on the outside, the way she was on the inside.

"Not that I'm not glad you're here," he said. "But, why, exactly, are you here, Dix?"

Dix. That was the second time he'd called her that. She liked it. She found it odd that no one had ever called her that before.

The smile she gave him felt strained. "I'm not sure. I came either to tell you goodbye or beg you to stay."

He gave a slight jerk, or a flinch, maybe. She couldn't tell. "Am I going somewhere?" he asked.

She took a sip and leaned back on the sofa. "I don't see any reason for you to stay now." When she slowly raised her gaze, she ran smack into his.

"I do." He held her gaze, trapped her.

She opened her mouth to speak, but her throat refused to work. She cleared it, then tried again. "You do what?"

He took a sip from his can without releasing her gaze. "See a reason to stay. I'm looking at it."

She couldn't breathe, couldn't move, couldn't swallow. It was becoming a habit around him, she thought inanely. "What's a woman supposed to say to a line like that?"

He gave her a crooked smile. "If you think it's just a line, then you obviously don't believe me."

They stared at each other for a long time, then finally Wade spoke. "All right, I'll go first. Right now I have no logical reason to stay in town. I can create one. A business opportunity has opened up here that I'd like to get my hands on. It would mean I'd be living here, in Tribute."

Dixie's heart raced. It soared. "What business?"

He shook his head. "I'm not ready to say, because as legitimate and promising and practical as that business would be, it's still only business. It wouldn't be the real reason I'd stay."

"It wouldn't?"

"You're going to make me say it, aren't you?"

Dixie started shaking. "Say what?"

"That I want to stay for *you*. I want you to want me to stay. I love you, Dixie. I know this is way too fast. We barely know each other. But for me, that doesn't seem to matter. If you say there's no chance for us, I'll pack up and go. But if you think—"

Dixie slammed her drink can onto the coffee table, leaped over the table and into Wade's arms. "Don't you dare," she cried, covering his face with kisses. "Don't you dare leave."

Wade squeezed his eyes shut and tried to breathe. "Thank God."

"I love you, I love you, I want you to stay." She held on tight and kissed him frantically, as if he were fading away in her arms.

"I didn't want to leave." He kissed her cheek, her chin, her neck. "But I didn't think I could stand to stay if you didn't want me."

"Not want you? I've been pining away for you for days."

He grinned down at her. "We can't have that. Here. Are you feeling faint?" He swept her up in his arms. His brow raised in question. "Maybe you need to lie down."

"Yes," she told him, her heart and her confidence swelling. "I most definitely need to lie down. But not alone. I'm so tired of alone."

He carried her into his small bedroom and stood

her beside the bed, then turned on the bedside lamp. "Ah, Dix." He cupped her face gently in both hands and looked into her eyes. "You don't ever have to lie down alone again."

Something—everything—inside Dixie stilled. "Ever?"

"Not if you marry me."

After she blinked to clear her vision, and swallowed around the sudden lump in her throat, Dixie placed her hand over his heart and felt the beating there. "I need to know that it's you asking me, you who feels this way, that this isn't some trick of your cellular memory."

"That's my heart you feel beating, and I've got the scar to prove it. What I thought or felt from cellular memory was for the boys. I never had a thought about you until I saw you that day I walked into the diner. This is all me, Dixie. Wade Harrison loves Dixie McCormick, and Wade Harrison loves her sons and Pops. Wade Harrison wants to marry all of you. As long as you're sure that you love me, and not just that heart you feel pounding away in there."

"Oh, it's you I love," she assured him. "If I was mixing you up with Jimmy Don, we'd already be divorced."

"That was fast. I think I missed our wedding. I know I missed our wedding night."

Dixie smiled and pulled him close, bumping her hips against his. "Why don't we see if we can do something about that?" She stepped back and reached to pull her T-shirt off over her head, but Wade stopped her.

"Let me."

Dixie shivered.

"Cold?"

She tried to laugh. "I think I'm nervous. I haven't done this in a while. A long while."

He gently raised her T-shirt and pulled it off. He tossed it to the floor. "Neither have I, but they say you never forget how. Look at you. I knew you'd be beautiful."

And she was, he thought. She was trim and tight, her muscles toned from keeping up with two boys, an old man, a business and hundreds of customers. His hand wasn't quite steady when he reached for the snap on her jeans.

She pushed his hands away. "My turn." She unbuttoned his shirt. Her fingers fumbled the job a couple of times, and it warmed him all the way through.

They stood there in the lamplight beside the bed, two people, both nervous, both eager, cherishing each other and the new love they'd found. When she opened his shirt and saw the long, thick scar down his chest, she nearly wept.

"I'm so sorry they had to do this to you. But I'm so grateful, too." She placed her hand over his heart and felt the strong, steady beat. "It's a good heart, for a good man."

Wade felt her words seep clear into his bones.

They finished undressing each other, and he took her down onto the bed, where he braced himself above her on his forearms. "Are you sure you want to do this?"

She met his gaze squarely, her heart, and her voice, filled with certainty. "Yes." She entwined her arms around his neck and pulled his lips toward hers. And finally...finally, they kissed.

Oh, he was sweet. Warm and darkly flavored, the way a man should be. She savored him with her lips and tongue, giving him all she had, all she was, trying to tell him with her kiss all the feelings she had for him but couldn't express in words.

He broke away from her mouth to taste her neck, her shoulder, her collarbone. The valley between her breasts. He teased her, kissing his way up one slope, down another, but never, never right on the tip, where she craved it. He trailed his tongue down to her navel, and lower. Then over the juncture of one thigh, then the other.

Someone was making small moaning sounds, and she was stunned to realize it was her. Suddenly she'd had all the torturous pleasure she could stand without returning the favor. She pushed Wade over and straddled his hips.

"My turn," she whispered. Then she kissed him, from head to toe. She started at his brow and moved on to his cheeks, his nose, but skipped his mouth. She might not be able to move on from there, and she didn't want to miss any part of him.

His skin was salty, his cheeks rough with five-o'clock shadow. His throat, such a strong throat. And sensitive, if his sharp intake of breath meant anything.

It was the scar she was after. She wanted to kiss it, somehow make it better. A smooth strip down the middle of his glorious chest.

Wade stayed as still as he could while she kissed his scar. The last woman who'd seen it, more than a year ago now, had turned up her nose and called it ugly. He'd put his shirt back on and taken her home. Hadn't seen her since. Any tiny sting left over from that episode melted away in the tender heat of Dixie's ministrations. She wasn't merely kissing it, she was tasting it with her tongue and her lips. Every ounce of blood in his body rushed to his groin.

Who would have thought a scar could become an erogenous zone?

Certainly not him, because thought was not possible as she reached the end of the scar and dipped her tongue into his navel. If she took that sweet, hot mouth of hers any farther down…

She didn't. She kissed her way back up his chest. She was kinder to him than he'd been to her, for she found his nipples and let her mouth play. Wade nearly reared off the bed, so exquisite was the sensation. By the time she moved to the second nipple, he was breathing hard and fast, and blood and heat pounded through his groin and he was ready to explode.

He rolled and took her with him until she lay

beneath him and he lay in the cradle of her thighs. "This," he managed between clenched teeth. "This is where I belong. Right here, with you."

"Yes," she whispered fiercely, her hips rising to meet his. "Yes. Yes. Yes."

Something inside them snapped. He locked his mouth on hers and they devoured each other. Tongues danced, lips and teeth nipped. Hands grasped, slipped on sweat-slicked skin. Hips thrust, hers to his, his to hers. Heat and tempo built until Dixie thought there was simply no more to feel. But she was wrong.

Wade trailed one hand along her hip, over, down, between her thighs. When he touched her, her back arched off the bed. She tried to bite back the cry of stunned pleasure. Too tame a word, *pleasure,* for what raced through her.

"Not without you," she moaned. "Please, I don't want to go without you."

"You won't. I'm with you all the way." He dipped a finger inside, felt her readiness to accept him. Settling his hips in place, he nudged at her opening. Then he was inside her, and nothing had ever felt so right. "Are you with me?"

She raised her knees to take him in deeper. "Yes. Oh, yes."

He began to move, and she moved with him. Long, slow thrusts at first that quickly sped to a breathless pace as they chased that first explosion together. And when it happened, Dixie called out his name, and he followed her off the edge of the world.

Wade was the first to stir. When his mind started functioning again, he pressed his lips to Dixie's neck and worried that he might be crushing her. He shifted his weight, but she wrapped her arms around his waist and made a small sound of protest.

He settled his hips, but kept his upper body weight braced on his forearms.

"I suppose," he said lazily, "since we've already agreed to get married, and now we've made love, it's probably a little late to concern ourselves with birth control."

Dixie meant to laugh pleasantly. But she was so sated, she didn't have the strength. It came out as a slight snicker. "You think?" she said. Then she patted his backside. "Not to worry. I'm on the pill."

He looked down at her, all tousled and sleepy-eyed, and smiled.

"You look pleased with yourself," she said.

"I'm pleased with both of us. I'm pleased with the whole wide world. I'm afraid that any minute I might burst out in song, and believe me, I don't have the voice for it. It'll scare you to death, and you'll call off the wedding. Then we'll discover that you got pregnant tonight, and the whole town will be talking about that unwed pregnant woman who slings hash at the diner."

Dixie heard his attempt at a Texas drawl and caught the gist of what he was saying and burst out laughing.

"What? You don't like my accent?"

"I'm trying to picture how to explain being pregnant and unmarried to Pops and the boys."

"Do you want to get pregnant?" He wasn't laughing now.

Suddenly neither was she. "Maybe. I've always wanted more children, but had pretty much decided that wasn't going to happen. But I'm not in a hurry. We've got time to decide. If you don't want anymore kids, I can live with that."

He gave her a crooked smile. "And if I want a dozen?"

"Then you better gather up several more wives, because I'm not giving you a dozen, unless they start coming in big batches."

"Like puppies?"

"That's right. A litter. Then we'd have a need for all that money of yours."

He stroked his finger down her nose. "Does my money really bother you so much?"

She lowered her gaze and combed her fingers through the hair on his chest. "I don't know. I don't know how much money you have. I've never had more than enough to get by on." Her eyes flew open. "You have to believe that I'm not after your money. Tell me you believe that."

"Of course I believe it. I'm not worried about that."

"I'll sign any prenup you want, I swear."

Wade smiled. "My father will think that's great. My mother and sisters will roll their eyes and think you have no sense, that you should have gotten me to guarantee specific funds to you if we break up, and I should support your children— What?"

"Your parents? Oh my God. What are they going to say about all of this?"

"This? You and me? They'll look at me and say, 'it's about damn time.' The thing they're going to raise their collective Harrison eyebrows at is the paper."

"What paper?"

"Well." He rolled off her and bunched up the pillows. They snuggled up side by side and he told her his plan. "You've heard that Bill Gray is retiring and selling the paper."

"No. I hadn't heard."

"You've been in the kitchen. You miss the good stuff in there."

"Don't I know it. Tomorrow I'm free! But what about the paper?"

"I'm going to make him an offer."

"You? A small-town newspaper?"

"Don't scoff at small-town newspapers. The entire Harrison Corporation and our personal family fortune began when my great-great-grandfather started a small-town weekly in Montana. I want to take the *Tribute Banner* and see what I can do with it. I want to edit it myself, manage it myself, the whole works. My father and sisters are going to be pea green with envy. My mother is going think I'm out of my mind, and then she's going to quietly have a stroke."

"Maybe you should talk it over with your family before you commit yourself to it."

"And maybe I shouldn't. This is something I want to do. I want to prove to myself that I can. I want to contribute something to this town. I want to live here, with you and our children—Ben and Tate and any others we might have—and Pops."

"Have you talked to Bill Gray yet?" she asked.

"No. Tomorrow morning. I can transfer some funds to the bank here."

"I'm sure they'll be glad to see you coming."

"I wouldn't replace any staff at the paper right off. Leave everything in place and see how it goes for a while. I'd just slip into Gray's place at first, take over the editorial, the managing, editing, whatever else he does. But that's for tomorrow. I guess you left Pops in charge at the house?"

"Yes, and I better be getting back before he sends the hounds out to find me."

"Aha. You don't have any hounds," he pointed out. "Which reminds me that I've always wanted a dog, so I'll probably be getting one, unless you have strong objections, in which case, we can negotiate."

She grinned. "A dog, huh? Anything else?"

"Guitar lessons. I always wanted to learn to play."

She laughed. "You can become the next Willie Nelson. Anything else?"

"Just one." He kissed the tip of her nose. "When do you want to get married?"

Dixie laughed and sat up, pulling the sheet up to cover her breasts.

"Going shy on me?"

"Why, Mr. Harrison, I barely know you."

Wade raised his brow. "Oh, I think you know me better than just about anyone else I can name." He grinned, pulling the sheet from her grasp. "It was spoiling my view. About that wedding date?"

"I don't have a clue," she said honestly. "Everything's happened so fast. First we have to tell our families."

"My family's first question is going to be, 'When?'"

"Hmm. You're right. It would be easier all around if we did it after the boys start back to school. That way, if we decide to take off a few days on a honeymoon, they can stay with classmates and some other poor woman won't have to watch them all day while they're in school. Business is lighter at the diner, then, too. September. The middle of the month?"

"Whenever you say. I'll be there. Do you want to do it up big, or fly to Vegas and get married in the Love Me Tender Wedding Chapel by an Elvis impersonator?"

"You made that up. Love Me Tender Wedding Chapel?"

He shrugged and smiled. "Whatever. Big, small or elope?"

"Won't your parents expect you to have a big wedding in New York?"

"No. They'll expect me to make my bride happy."

"Oh. Well, then. That's easy. Kiss me."

He did. Thoroughly. It was two in the morning before he walked her home.

Pops saw them coming up the drive, hand in hand. He saw the way they stopped, looked at each other. The way they kissed. His vision blurred.

"You can rest easy, Jimmy Don. You done good."

Epilogue

September 14
Tribute Park
Tribute, Texas

Nearly half the town had turned out for the dedication ceremony. Dixie was beside herself with curiosity. So was Pops. Ben and Tate were wild. They knew the new monument had something to do with their dad. That would be their *real* dad, not the new stepdad they were getting the very next day when their mom and Wade got married.

Wade was nervous and trying not to show it. The

nerves, he knew, were a sign of how important the community acceptance and approval of this monument was to him. He'd worked tirelessly these past few months, researching town records, talking to residents, coming up with the names and circumstances of other local people who'd done heroic deeds outside of war. Ordinary citizens who'd committed extraordinary acts.

Between working on that and taking over as the new owner, publisher and editor-in-chief of the *Tribute Banner,* and spending time with his future family, he'd been…what was it they said around here? Busy as a one-armed paperhanger. Or maybe, busy as a one-legged man at a butt-kicking contest?

The latter seemed more unfortunate than busy, but he would get the hang of this Texas talk, eventually. To brush up on his skills, he turned to his parents, who, along with his sisters and their families, had come down to see Wade and Dixie get married tomorrow, and said, "How y'all doing?"

His father chortled.

His sisters laughed.

His nieces and nephews mimicked him in singsong voices. "How y'all doin'? How y'all doin'? Y'all. Y'all. Y'all."

Wade's mother gave Dixie a mock glare. "Did you teach him that?" Mrs. Harrison demanded.

"Who, me?" Dixie claimed innocently, with a hand to her chest. Then she leaned closer to her future mother-in-law. "You're getting a kick out of this. Admit it."

Myrna Harrison's lips quirked. "I'll do no such thing, daughter."

On the riser built beside the new monument for the occasion came a loud squeal of speakers not adjusted properly. "Ladies and gentlemen!" called the mayor. "It's time to begin, so corral the kids and gather round. I'm sure you've noticed the new sign renaming this area more fittingly as Tribute Park. You've all seen and shared in the pride of the two monuments to our war dead on the other side of the park. Always we honor those who give the ultimate sacrifice so that we might live in freedom.

"But a person need not be in a war to be a hero. Sometimes, an ordinary citizen is called upon to do the extraordinary and steps forth to accomplish it without complaint. These heroes, too, must be honored and remembered. Today, thanks to a private endowment, we dedicate this new monument to our civilian heroes.

"We've researched in detail to come up with the names of people we believe belong on this memorial, but I'm sure there are some we missed. If any of you know of someone who's done something truly heroic, write down what they did and why they belong on this monument and send it to city hall. All decisions as to inclusion are made by the town council."

Wade wiped his damp palms along the thighs of

his jeans. A moment later he felt Dixie's small hand slip into his and squeeze. He looked down into those blue, blue eyes and felt the encouragement she offered in those eyes, in her hand, in her smile.

She hadn't seen the monument yet. No one had except the workmen. Even Wade hadn't seen it. He'd created the concept on paper. The council had approved the drawing and the granite he'd suggested. But he hadn't seen the finished product, and it was killing him.

"Ladies and gentlemen," said the mayor, "I give you the Tribute Wall."

One of the council members pulled on a rope, and the canvas covering that hid the monument rose up and back to reveal a five-foot-high by twelve-feet-long curving wall of smoky granite. Carved top center ran the words: Tribute to Heroes. Similar to other memorials, it was divided into several equal-size panels.

The first name on the first panel was Melba Throckmorton, a local schoolteacher whose heroic efforts saved a classroom of students from a deadly tornado, at much risk to herself, in 1901.

Next came a grocer named Wendell Stoklasa. In 1923, unarmed, he faced down armed bank robbers to shield a pregnant woman whom he'd never met. He took the bullet meant for her. He survived the ordeal, but lost his leg as a result.

There were a couple of others listed, but Wade

pulled Dixie and their families to the second panel. Wade stood in front of the wording so no one could see, and motioned to someone in the back of the crowd.

Dixie turned to look but didn't recognize the strangers, two men and a woman, who came to stand beside him.

"Dixie, Pops, Ben, Tate, I'd like you to meet some newfound friends of mine. This is Harvey Willard, John Bates and Justine Adams. And now—"

"But, Wade, who—"

"Just read, Dix. Just read."

So, Dixie read.

Because of his generosity and courage, in 2004 James Donald McCormick saved the lives of five people, gave sight to a sixth and made the lives of four others infinitely more livable. He was an organ donor. Justine Adams, John Bates, Wade Harrison, Martin Letterman and Harvey Willard thank you, Jimmy Don, for their lives. Constance Easly thanks you for her sight. Kim Jenkins, Patricia Bardo, Eve Miles, and Pete Richmond thank you for the grafts and ligaments you donated. You're our hero.

Wade read every word twice, making sure there'd been no mistakes. Then he turned to Dixie.

She stood with both hands over her mouth, tears

streaming down her face. "Oh, Wade. It's…it's wonderful. Pops? Do you see?"

Pops saw but couldn't speak.

"Boys." Dixie put a hand on the back of each of their necks. "Can you read all that? That's your dad. See? Your dad's a genuine hero. It says so right there on the new wall."

"Golly." Ben's eyes were huge.

"For real?" Tate asked, slightly confused.

"For real," Dixie assured him.

Wade's mother stepped forward and kissed her son on the cheek. "I'm so proud of you for doing this."

"Thanks, Mom."

Dixie led the boys over to the other transplant recipients and told them these were their donor's sons. There were handshakes and hugs and tears. And the inevitable laughter that comes when children are involved.

"You got my dad's liver?" Tate asked Mr. Bates.

"Yes, son, I did, and it saved my life, so I'm mighty grateful to your dad."

"Listen up, folks," Pops said loudly to their little group of family and friends. "Wade's done a fine thing, getting this memorial built for the folks who deserve to be remembered. We're all proud of him for doing it, proud of Jimmy Don for deserving it. Now, that's enough of this gloomy-Gus sad stuff. These two young folks, Dixie and Wade, are getting married tomorrow. I say we go get us a good supper over at the diner, then rest up for the big day."

Wade leaned over and whispered in Pops's ear. "Good going. Thanks."

Pops, with Ben and Tate in tow, led the way out of the park and down the block to Dixie's Diner. Trailing behind the large group of McCormicks and Harrisons, way behind, Wade and Dixie held hands and gazed into each other's eyes.

"I love you," he told her.

"And I love you," she answered.

"Let's get married tomorrow."

"Yes. Let's."

And they did.

* * * * *

Look for the next book in the compelling miniseries
TRIBUTE, TEXAS
by Janis Reams Hudson
FINDING NICK
A reporter comes to Tribute looking for an
elusive firefighter and finds there's more to
the man than meets the eye....
On sale August 2006
Available wherever Silhouette books are sold.

Page-turning drama...

Exotic, glamorous locations...

Intense emotion and passionate seduction...

Sheikhs, princes and billionaire tycoons...

This summer, may we suggest:

**THE SHEIKH'S
DISOBEDIENT BRIDE**

by Jane Porter

On sale June.

**AT THE GREEK TYCOON'S
BIDDING**

by Cathy Williams

On sale July.

**THE ITALIAN MILLIONAIRE'S
VIRGIN WIFE**

On sale August.

With new titles to choose from every month,
discover a world of romance in our books written
by internationally bestselling authors.

Hotel Marchand

**Four sisters.
A family legacy.
And someone is out to destroy it.**

**A captivating new limited
continuity, launching June 2006**

The most beautiful hotel in New Orleans,
and someone is out to destroy it. But mystery,
danger and some surprising family revelations
and discoveries won't stop the Marchand sisters
from protecting their birthright…
and finding love along the way.

This riveting new saga begins with

by national bestselling author

JUDITH ARNOLD

The party at Hotel Marchand is in full swing when the lights suddenly go out. What does head of security Mac Jensen do first? He's torn between two jobs—protecting the guests at the hotel and keeping the woman he loves safe.

A woman to protect. A hotel to secure. And no idea who's determined to harm them.

On Sale June 2006

HMITD

COMING NEXT MONTH

#1765 THE RELUCTANT CINDERELLA—Christine Rimmer
Talk of the Town
When humble business owner Megan Schumacher landed the Banning's department store account, she landed Greg Banning, too. He loved her ideas for updating the company's image—and couldn't get the image of this sexy woman out of his head. But the town gossips had a field day—and Greg's ex-wife, who'd introduced the pair, *wasn't* amused....

#1766 PRINCESS IN DISGUISE—Lilian Darcy
Wanted: Outback Wives
Tired of her philandering fiancé, jet-setting Princess Misha decided to unwind at a remote sheep farm in Australia. But when she arrived, farmer Brant Smith mistook her for one of the candidates a local woman's magazine had been sending him as a possible wife! Perhaps the down-to-earth royal fit the bill more than either of them first suspected....

#1767 THE BABY TRAIL—Karen Rose Smith
Baby Bonds
Finding a stranger's baby in her sunroom, Gwen Longworthy resolved to reunite mother and child, since she knew all too well the pain of separation. Luckily she had former FBI agent Garrett Maxwell to help search for the mother...and soothe Gwen's own wounded heart.

#1768 THE TENANT WHO CAME TO STAY—Pamela Toth
Reunited
Taking in male boarder Wade Garrett was a stretch for Pauline Mayfield—falling in love with him really turned heads! And just when Pauline had all the drama she could take, her estranged sister, Lily, showed up, with child in tow and nowhere to go. The more the merrier...or would Lily get up to her old tricks and make a play for Pauline's man?

#1769 AT THE MILLIONAIRE'S REQUEST—Teresa Southwick
When millionaire Gavin Spencer needed a speech therapist for his injured son, he asked for M. J. Taylor's help. But the job reminded M.J. of the tragic loss of her own child, and her proximity to Gavin raised trust issues for them both. As the boy began to heal, would M.J. and Gavin follow suit—and give voice to their growing feelings for each other?

#1770 SECOND-TIME LUCKY—Laurie Paige
Canyon Country
How ironic that family counselor Caileen Peters had so much trouble keeping her own daughter in line. And that Caileen was turning to her client Jefferson Aquilon, a veteran raising two orphans, for help. But mother and daughter both found inspiration in the Aquilon household—and Caileen soon found something more in Jefferson's arms.

SSECNM0606

SPECIAL EDITION